I0573793

The Prettiest Girl
I Ever Killed

Published in electronic format by
PROLOGUE BOOKS
an imprint of F+W Media, Inc.
10151 Carver Road
Blue Ash, Ohio 45242
www.prologuesbooks.com

eISBN 10: 1-4405-3902-2
eISBN 13: 978-1-4405-3902-2

POD ISBN 10: 1-4405-5618-0
POD ISBN 13: 978-1-4405-5618-0

This is a work of fiction. Names, characters, corporations, institutions, organizations, events,
or locales in this novel are either the product of the author's imagination or, if real, used
fictitiously. The resemblance of any character to actual persons (living or dead) is entirely
coincidental.

This work has been previously published in print format by:
Gold Medal Books.

The Prettiest Girl I Ever Killed

Charles Runyon

PROLOGUE BOOKS

F+W Media, Inc.

PROLOGUE

The name of the game is Death.

Most people play without knowing, like sleepwalkers dancing to slow faint music. A few play with full awareness of the game and its inevitable end. Bernice Struble thought she was playing the adultery game, but I taught her that it was only a variation of The Death Game.

I noticed that she'd started coming into town every day between nine and eleven a.m. Her husband was at the depot getting ready for the ten o'clock freight. After it left, he'd be clearing up cargo and checking bills.

Bernice did no shopping; met no friends. By the tenth day my interest was engaged. I watched her park at the curb and sit smoking a cigaret. One plump arm lay along the window. Her short fingers beat a desultory tattoo on the side of the car. Her lips looked swollen and sensuous as they pursed and pulled on the white cylinder. Her eyes were moist and hot, measuring the men as they passed. After a time she got out of her car, flipped her cigaret into the gutter, and strolled along the two blocks which made up the business district of Sherman. She carried her bosom high and forward, with its salient points clearly etched against her white-and-green print dress. I watched her amble past the Square Deal grocery store, past the Purina feed store, Grant's Recreation Parlor and Pool Hall, Stubb's Tavern, Slavitt's Repair Shop and Auto Salvage. She cut left just before she reached the schoolhouse. As she crossed the highway toward the park, the sun reflected off white gravel and gave her dress a brief transparency. In five years she'd be coarse and dumpy, but now she had no need to stretch and compress her flesh with latex and elastic. The soft rolling shape beneath Bernice's dress was Bernice; she was dealing it straight, letting you know in advance, and if you were disappointed later it was your own fault for not looking.

In the park she sat on the wooden steps of the weather-blackened bandstand, cooled by the shade of gigantic elms. It was a hot day in late June; already the thermometer had topped ninety. She smoked another cigaret, then rose, walked across the grass, got into her car and drove out of town. The Strubles had twenty acres and a house two miles east of town. I waited a half hour and no cars followed. I wondered: Was it a mating ritual, or was she simply a woman with nothing to do? She had no close friends in town; a depot agent with two-year tenure never becomes part of a Missouri farm community. Her husband was a mild young man with a taste for beer and a passion for shuffleboard. I weighed the risk and found it non-existent. I got in my car and drove west, then I cut back and took the old south road across the river, drove east two miles and came back toward town on the blacktop. I turned south on the Braden Gravel and reached their house, an old-fashioned two-story structure with tall narrow windows.

She was sitting in her front yard on a plaid blanket drinking a glass of red Kool-aid. I pulled off onto the track worn beside the mailbox and called: "Where's Bill?"

She rose from the blanket and came forward.

"He's at the depot," she said, opening the wooden gate. She negotiated the plank laid across the grader ditch and came up to the car, resting her forearms along the open window. "He don't come back till around noon. He meets the ten o'clock, then he goes up to Stubb's and has a beer, so he don't come home till around noon."

Her face held no expression. Her two front teeth were prominent; not protruding, but larger than the others. I noticed streaks of flour on her dress where she'd wiped her hands after baking. I felt a pulse of excitement; she'd been in her kitchen cooking something for her man, and here I was about to...

It was hard to keep from breaking into a foolish grin. "Won't be home until noon, eh?"

"No." It's hard to convey the exact tone of her voice. It showed no coyness, no arch, teasing flirtation. She was like a child saying, *I want ...*

"You want to take a ride?"

I think she'd already made up her mind; she glanced up the road toward the main highway, then opened the door and slid into the car. I'd just pulled out onto the gravel when she said: "I didn't bring my cigarets."

"I've got some."

Thirty seconds later she pointed to a dirt road leading toward the river. "You can turn in there."

When we were bouncing along the track beneath the cotton woods, I glanced over at her. Beads of perspiration gleamed in the fine white hairs of her upper lip. Despite her neutral tone, she was excited; this was the only adventure she knew.

Before we reached the river she pointed to a thicket of willows. "There," she said. A breathy tautness had altered her voice.

I killed the engine and set the brake. As she got out of the car I asked: "Who'd you come here with before?"

She shook her head. "That'd be telling."

"Point is, he might show up."

"Huh-uh. He left the country."

Then I knew who it was: Wayne Bergen, a truck driver who delivered gas and diesel fuel to neighboring farms. A tall, easygoing bag of bones with an insolent manner, he'd been fired two weeks ago for getting drunk on the job—just before Bernice started showing up in town....

She led me twenty yards into the thicket and stopped in a small clearing. Floodwaters had heaped a dune of sand behind a fallen cottonwood. Wild grapes and elderberries draped the tall trees and wrist-thick willows screened us from all sides.

"Keep these for me," she said, shoving her panties in my pocket. "If we hear anyone, I'll roll into the weeds and you can say you chased a rabbit in here."

There were a few kisses, but hardly worth mentioning, like the playing of "The Star-Spangled Banner" before a prizefight. There was also sand and airless heat and mosquitoes. The girl had energy but no art; heat but no style. She seemed to have the nervous system of a dinosaur; one small brain controlling the lower portion of her body, and another in her head. Her face remained the same throughout, eyes closed and mouth open, sweat dewing her upper lip, like a restless child dreaming on a hot afternoon. Poor dumb broad, she had nothing working for her but an extra helping of hormones. I felt like most of me was unnecessary. She'd thrown out her line and I was the fish who'd struck the bait; she'd been sitting there in the yard with the house locked up and it hadn't mattered who came by, Stubby or the banker or Earless Joe who racked balls in the pool hall....

When it was over she shook the sand from her dress and said that if we came again she'd remember the blanket. I knew there'd be a next time, because I had something to make up with her; she'd used me, and according to the rules of the game, she qualified as a victim.

We managed to meet about twice a week. Bernice was addicted to rituals; when I didn't show for three days, she'd come to town and do her invitational walk around the square. So I'd get in my car and drive out. She'd be standing at the front gate as though waiting for the mailman to deliver a package. If there was any traffic on the road, I drove on and came back later. If the road was clear, Bernice got in and crouched beneath the dash until we reached the willows. She went ahead while I waited to make sure nobody had followed. I'd convinced her there was reason to be scared and she loved it. With the truck driver she'd been an animal crawling off under the bushes. Now she was risking all for love, like the heroines of the true confessions she read while waiting for me. This amused me because basically she was a neat little German *Hausfrau*. She used to fold her dress up neatly across her belly so it wouldn't wrinkle. Once I tore her panties, pulling them from my pocket; suddenly I was no longer custodian of her lingerie; she just didn't wear them when she expected me. I'd approach the mailbox and think of her standing there with her legs going up and up without interruption, and my mouth would get dry....

But she was too simple, and by September I'd lost interest in the sex game. The less interest I showed, the more she tried, and the more bored I became....

I watched it spiral up and up; I gave her money and that put the whole affair on a new footing. She was puzzled; I told her to buy herself a dress or something. But we no longer met for mutual pleasure. I kept giving her money, and she strained to pay it off in the only coin she had. But when you try, you can't.

Our last meeting in the willows in October was cramped and shivery, and I said we'd better end it. She said:

"I'll find a place we can meet inside. Don't talk about ending it."

Her dinosaur brain must have been stimulated by need, because she set it up beautifully. I only followed instructions. I drove by her mailbox and she gave me the sign from her window. I parked the car by the willows and walked along the river until I reached their property line. Then I approached the house under cover of a hedgerow. This brought me to the rear of the house. Down three steps, through a door, and I was in the basement. The furnace kept it warm; the presence of her washing machine and clothes hung up to dry filled it with a miasma of soap and wet fabrics. After I was in, she locked the door to the basement. The connubial couch was a rubber air mattress laid down behind the furnace. She asked me if it wasn't better than the thicket and I told her it smelled like a laundry. She said she felt more secure here, and to prove it she undressed for the first time. She walked around, her bare feet leaving damp tracks on the dusty concrete. She wanted me to say something, but I could only wonder how long it would take that blazing furnace to consume her flesh. I wondered if she would swell and burst like a hot dog; if the dark blonde hair would sizzle and shrink to a black kinky mass. In my mind's eye I saw the victim's hat on her head: a black skullcap with a tiny red tassel, like a Talmudic scholar's. Mine was a wide-brimmed corsair hat with an ostrich plume. You've got to have style or the Watcher gets bored. Without style you're only a butcher.

But the rules of the game required a motive, and she hadn't yet given me one. I beckoned her to join me on the air mattress. She strained to please me and afterward she gave me a piece of apple pie. She wanted a pat on the head but I gave her money and she looked like she was going to cry....

The excitement of bringing the game into enemy camp held my interest until mid-December, but the strain was wearing down Bernice. She started complaining about her husband:

"You know I don't like him to touch me any more, but that only gets him worked up. Sometimes he comes out from the depot after the midnight train and wakes me up with his damn poking; or it's after the six a.m. train and he comes in while I'm fixing breakfast and runs his hand up my dress.

It's all I can do to keep from hitting him."

Another time: "Why don't we take off together? Don't say you can't. You'd find a way if you had to."

And finally: "I've waited for you to do something, but you didn't. So I went ahead and did it."

I felt the skin draw tight across my cheekbones. "Did what?"

"I saved the money you gave me. I told my husband I was going to visit my sister in Minneapolis. But instead I'm going to Las Vegas and get a divorce. You can meet me there and we'll get married."

"I can't leave here."

"You'll have to when I tell Bill what's been happening."

I heard a high, faint buzzing in my cars. I thought, with a mild, remote sort of interest: Well, well, look at what I've built, a little death machine. I said:

"Your word against mine."

"Is it? Remember the day you couldn't come? You put the note in my mailbox. I've still got it."

"Unsigned."

"But in your handwriting."

Suddenly I was outside the game; I saw all the pieces strung out on the board below me. I'd put the note in her box without being aware of any ulterior motive; now I saw that my subconscious had been leading me into a trap.

"Wait a few days," I said. "I'll think it over."

"Two days," she said. Something in the German countenance limits expression to either arrogance or servility; there's no middle ground. Bernice's face was wearing the arrogance; now it dissolved into servile apology. "I don't want it this way. You forced me into it."

I smiled, because she didn't know how true that was.

For two days I tried to plan. A car accident... gas... something with the furnace... burn down the house.

My intellect couldn't help trying to take charge even though I knew it was wrong to plan. If the time is right, everything will be laid out. You just assemble the pieces, like a model plane with each part numbered.

When I arrived two days later there it was: The packing had worn out in their electric pump; the cover was off the well and the pump removed to the shop. Meanwhile water had to be drawn up with a bucket attached to a rope. The morning was cold and clear; telephone wires hummed and the sun was a pale disc which gave light but no heat. As I went in, I noticed that ice had frozen around the curb of the well. Beside the basement door stood the tools they'd used to remove the pump.

I told Bernice I'd decided to go with her, and we spent a quarter hour discussing plans. She prepared to consummate the deal on the air mattress but I said no. I knew that if there was an autopsy, the fact that she'd just had intercourse would be hard to explain.

"I'd like a drink of water before I go," I said.

"I'll get it from the refrigerator."

"It would taste better from the well."

She frowned. "We might be seen."

"I'll just be getting a drink of water. Anyway, does it matter? Your husband has to know sooner or later."

That reminded her that she had reason to please me, no matter how ridiculous my request. Her felt house-slippers skidded on the ice as she walked to the well. I was behind her, holding a massive pipe wrench I'd taken from inside the door. I waited until she'd pulled the bucket almost to the top, then I called her name.

She turned. In the moment it took her to focus her eyes on my face, she saw the wrench. I watched the awful knowledge come into her eyes; it was a puzzled kind of sadness. Her jaw dropped as I brought the wrench down. My footing was bad and I managed only a glancing blow on her left temple. She dropped the rope and tried to scramble away, skittering on the ice like a hog on a frozen pond. I swung again and caught her behind the ear. She fell across the curbing, dazed but not out. I put my foot against her shoulder and tried to push her into the well. Her hands clawed at the icy bricks and her short crimson nails held like talons. I brought the wrench down with all my strength. The impact jolted it from my hand, but the blow was good. She dropped headfirst like a bomb from a bomb bay. Cool air puffed up into my face as she went down; her legs were bare and she'd prepared for the as usual. That was a pathetic and touching sight, and the last I saw of her. She struck with a hollow *Chung!* and the bottom of the well exploded into a thousand darting splinters of light. I watched the water until it was a bright silver coin, then I returned to the basement. I cleaned up the cigaret butts and threw them into the furnace. In her bedroom I found her purse; I took out the money she'd been saving and put it in my wallet. I found the note I'd given her and threw it in the furnace. I took the water pitcher from the refrigerator and carried it out to the well. I poured water over the flecks of blood and watched it turn to mush as it froze. I set the pitcher on the curb so it would appear that she'd come out to fill it. I wanted her found quickly; I wanted no mysteries, no inquiries. I thought of the wrench and decided it must be lying at the bottom of the well—unless it had somehow gotten tangled in Bernice's dress. If that had happened... tough. You can't anticipate those things.

I felt calm as I followed the hedgerow back to the river. My crepe-soled shoes left no mark on the frozen ground. There was no way they could trace me; nobody was even aware that I knew her.

She made number ten. I searched myself for elation and found none. It was like reaching into a cookie jar and finding nothing. I was empty.

Later it came, of course. Not elation, but a sort of remembrance. I thought of Bernice and her little *Hausfrau* attitudes: the way she gathered up the tissues and cigaret butts which had accumulated during my visit, bending from the waist and snatching them up like a hen snapping up grains of corn... opening the furnace door with face pinched tight and throwing the little package away with a gesture of rejection... then looking to see if she'd missed anything, biting her index finger with those two prominent incisor teeth. I thought of her brain and its memories of me, now dead. (Within three days she'd been taken from the well, and reburied in her home town nearly two hundred miles away. The well was filled up, and her death ruled accidental.) I thought of the hours she'd spent waiting for me, the hope that must have surged up when she saw me, the habit she'd acquired of washing and perfuming herself in intimate places... something she would not have done if it hadn't been for me. Before she died I had changed her life. In a sense, I had created her....

I have only contempt for those who go out on a dark street and select a victim at random. They are ending a life they do not understand; they are crude and barbarous vandals, like savages who smash a radio. Let an engineer destroy a radio, that is significant. Let him destroy a radio which he has built himself, that is better still.

Bernice had lived her life. At twenty-one she was complete. She couldn't grow into something else, no more than a calf can grow into a gazelle; the genetic materials are not available. Bernice could only have become an older, coarser version of what she was; I could do nothing more with the materials at hand, so I destroyed her.

As weeks passed, the memory of Bernice became a sick sweetness, as when you eat too much pork fat. By killing Bernice, I seemed to have killed myself. I had existed in her mind, and when her mind ceased to exist... what became of the man she knew? I walked the street feeling my feet thud against the concrete and I would wonder whose feet they were. Walls began to waver, as in the heat warp from a stove. I worked harder, fitting my days with labor, creating things I could look at and somehow see myself reflected in—

But these things were only wood and metal and plants rising from the soil. I needed a person, a woman—not in a physical way, but as a partner in the game. My thoughts turned, as they often had before, to Velda.

I can walk past the store and see her behind the counter. Usually the store is empty, and she is alone. This quiet woman in this quiet place fascinates me. I stop and took through the plate glass, most of me hidden by posters Scotch-taped to the inside which announce sales on meat, soap powder and canned goods. An open book lies on the counter before her. She sits on a high stool, one bare knee atop the other, running the point

of her pencil through the pale rust-colored hair which she has pulled
above her ears and bound up in the back. From time to time she shifts her
legs, hooking one foot behind the ankle of the other. She is beautiful in a
way which does not immediately strike the eye: her features are almost,
but not quite, ordinary: a sheen of gold brightens her red-blonde hair, an
emerald tone deepens the green of her eyes; her narrow nose ends in a
slight upward tilt; her long smooth jaw suggests a masculine stubbornness.
Her upper lip forms a tight unmoving line; the lower swells and protrudes
slightly. She lights a cigaret without interrupting her reading, thrusting
out her jaw and lilting her head so that the lighter does not flare into her
eyes. She draws deeply once and allows the smoke to roll from her nose
and lips; then she deposits the cigaret in an ashtray and smokes it no more,
only waves away the wisps of smoke which trail across the page.

She does not look her thirty-five years: her body seems to have early
acquired a toughness, a resilience which resists the sagging effects of age.
Her long crossed thighs show faint ridges of muscle through the dress; her
calves are smoothly rounded, free of blue swollen veins which are the stig-
ma of the retail trade. She wears a bibbed white apron over a blue cotton
dress; her breasts press full and firm against it.

A customer enters; a bell rings above the door. She closes the book and
marks it with a sliver of cardboard; she slides off the stool and stands erect,
placing her palms flat on the wooden counter. A diamond-crusted circlet
glitters on her third finger, left hand; the large center stone shoots out
arrows of blue light. The customer is a talkative woman. Velda converses
with her: she laughs—a half-amused chuckle which ripples only the surface—she carries her verbal share of the conversation... but always there is
something reserved, some little chamber of emotion she does not open.
(The local people have forgotten that she is beautiful; they have seen her
so often they no longer see her. A woman comes to town only half as lovely as Velda and all heads turn to follow her because she is new. In a year
or two she will also become invisible, condemned to the peculiar anonymity a small town conveys.) Probably this is good for Velda, for she has
acquired none of the self-conscious poses of women who are accustomed
to attention. She has no false modesty because she knows no reason to feel
proud.

All this is speculation. I don't really know her—though I know her as
well as or better than anyone else in Sherman, because I have studied her
and they have not. At midmorning she often disappears behind the green
plywood partition which segregates her office and a small bathroom. She
locks the door and remains for sometimes an hour. I wonder what she does
in there, but the bell over the front door always rings when I enter. Even
when I muffle its ringing—as I did once by winding tape around the clap-
per—the wooden floor creaked and she came out looking flushed and sur-

prised. (Does she know I am studying her now? Probably not, I am a familiar face; my behavior undergoes no major change, and in minor changes I am shielded by the same anonymity which protects everyone else in this town.) Oh, I'm not teased by the mystery of what women *do* when they're alone... little dabs of grooming, searching out gray hairs, pushing hair masses here and there to see how it would look in a different style, checking for new pimples and wrinkles, squeezing blackheads... But what does she *see* when she looks in the mirror? What image is reflected to her and why does it dissatisfy her? Because there is discontent in the way the lips sometimes curve downward. It could be her marriage, but then she would need only to give some sign of availability and the men would come. Strangers make overtures, true, which she studies and rejects. The rejection is not important, but the study is. She desires, she does not obtain....

Another symptom is her reading. New worlds inside the covers of books. Surrogate experience, proving that reality falls short. Like any avid reader she knows words, good words, big ones. But, living in cultural isolation, she often mispronounces them, or drops them in the middle of a sentence, like a rock which destroys the symmetry of her speech. Her information is spotty, another result of undisciplined reading. She discovers history and devours all she can find on the subject, at the same time lacking even a high school graduate's knowledge of astronomy or philosophy. She is a strange blend of knowledge and naïveté. Normally she talks in a studied, level tone, letting no emotion out, merely communicating. Yet when she is angry, the blunt country words break through, pungent and steaming and barbed with the directness of the hills. The emerald eyes sparkle with green fire, the lips stretch tight across even white teeth, and you see that the words belong to her. You see her as she was when I first saw her, sitting in the back of a Studebaker wagon, her bare feet swinging a foot above the dusty road. She was a woodland creature born and raised in the hills of Brush Creek, taking her first look—not really, but it seemed so—at neon lights and movies and fountain Cokes. She was no beauty then; she had vivid freckles dusted across her cheekbones and the bridge of her nose. Her teeth were small and not quite closed up, with dark gaps between them. Her sunbleached hair was a hue most accurately described as mustard. It framed a long thin face which may have been clean when she started to town, but had since acquired a gray coating of road dust. She wore a dress made from a flowered Parina sack; it lay not quite flat across her chest; her immature breasts did not bounce with the movement of the wagon....

Now she is by local standards a rich man's wife. Nylon sheathes the legs which knew only wool in winter and the wind in summer. She has grown used to imported silk and French perfume and gold which does not turn green; her small hands know the satiny smoothness of new money and the wheel of the powerful, expensive car....

But this latter woman is totally divorced from the poor little hill girl. Velda is either one or the other, she is never a blend of the two.

I see her as a victim. This is as natural as a beautician seeing her with her head beneath a dryer, a policeman seeing her behind bars, or a surgeon seeing her with her stomach cut open. I think of how she would look dead, or in the process of being killed. (She would fight, this is certain; I visualize her as a naked, clawing, spitting savage.) But the picture is unsatisfactory, because she is not ready. Even at thirty-five, she is an unformed, immature woman.

An element is missing, a catalyst which will blend the hill girl with the rich man's wife and make her complete. The element is not me, for I am already in her life, and have blunted my power to affect her without risk. The element is not even in Sherman, for she has adapted to all those who live here, examined them and shoved then aside. The element must come from outside. Until she changes, Velda is immune....

CHAPTER ONE
Velda's Game

When you see a stranger in our town, you know he's come *here*, he's not passing through on his way to somewhere else. Sherman is the end, the jump-off. At the east side of town there's a sign reading: *State Maintenance Ends*. From here west the gravel roads dwindle away into a wilderness of limestone ridges they call the Brush Creek Nation. Ten miles west the ridges slope down into Lake Pillybay, but tourists always approach it from the other side on Highway 30.

That's why I stared at the man who came into the store just after I'd opened. A blond beard hid the lower part of his face; his deep tan was a rarity in late March. I watched him wipe mud from calf-high rubber boots and walk toward the counter. He was young, I could tell from the springy sureness of his walk. He was married; I saw the gold wedding band as he lay his palms flat on the counter. A deep bass voice asked for a can of Velvet and I set it in front of him. He opened it, gouged the tobacco with a long forefinger, and raised it to his nose. He squinted at me over the can and said:

"Velda Groenfelder?"

I shook my head. "Velda Bayrd. I married Louis Bayrd."

His sun-whitened eyebrows rose. "Ah, you've risen in the world. A flat-lander by marriage."

I frowned at him, looking for a familiar face beneath the beard. Only a native would speak of flatlanders with that peculiar taunting inflection.

"You used to live in the Nation?" I asked.

He nodded. There was movement behind the foliage as though he might be smiling, but I wasn't sure. I tilted my head so I could see his face in better light. That mat of beard darkened from yellow on his cheeks to a coppery black beneath his chin. A deep tan gave his blue eyes a piercing brilliance. He might have looked mean but I didn't feel it because of the intelligence in his eyes. Hate and intelligence don't go together.

I shrugged and smiled. "I can't place you. Come out from behind the bush."

like it. I saw something in his eyes I'd missed the first time I'd looked; a
hard reckless indifference. I knew the grin was there now, but it was a
twisted taunting thing that said I could think and do what I liked because
he didn't give a damn.

I took the can of tobacco and set it on the cash register.

"They sell tobacco in the tavern," I told him. "It's fresher. You'll like it better."

He shook his head slowly. "After fifteen years, Velda? I didn't even think
you'd know me."

"I knew your family. Your brother."

He leaned back, still smiling in a way that didn't reach his eyes, smiling
like I was a little doll doing all kinds of funny tricks.

"My brother Frank," he said. "Your sister Anne. She's been dead twelve
years and Frankie's serving life. And what's all that got to do with you and
me?"

"You know damn well what it's got to do with us."

"Code of the hills? The pride of the clan?" He shook his head. "I'm a long
time away from cornbread and hominy grits, Velda. I'm surprised you
aren't."

I felt hot blood burning my cheeks; I didn't like the way he made my
words sound. "They held a trial. The verdict was guilty."

"You believe it?"

"—Yes."

"All right. Stick to it. Don't even think about it." He reached past me and
picked up the tobacco; I could have stopped him by grabbing his hand, but
I couldn't make myself touch him. He dropped a quarter on the counter
and walked away. I was surprised to see that he was over six feet tall and
heavy in the shoulders. I remembered him as being thin and pale... but
then he'd only been sixteen when he left.

My hand touched the quarter and I started to ring it up. A sudden
impulse made me throw it toward the front of the store. It clanged against
the window and went spinning off, leaving a tiny starburst on the plate
glass. Curt paused an instant, then turned around.

"I suppose Frankie killed Bernice Struble too."

"Bernice? Why... that was an accident. The coroner's jury—"

"Keep believing it, Velda. The authorities are never wrong."

He smiled and walked out. I watched him climb into a mud-caked Ford
with a Florida license. His smile was gone now. He backed out and drove
away without looking back.

I went into the bathroom and bathed my face in cold water. I put my
hand to my breast and breathed slowly, wishing I'd inherited a little less
of the Groenfelder temper. I should have been dignified and haughty with
Curt: *Really, Mr. Friedland, did you expect to be met by a brass band?*

I touched up my lips and brushed back the red-blonde hair above my ears. Then I walked back into the empty store, through the warm smell of oranges and floor wax and leafy vegetables. I looked at the calendar: March twenty-third. I pulled a pencil from above my ear and circled it. It's a habit of mine; my husband says I try to hold back time by putting little traps around the dates. I saw that I'd also circled February tenth, the day Bernice Struble fell in the well....

Or was pushed? Oh no, I thought, I won't let Curt Friedland's evil seed take root. The coroner's report had said she died by drowning. Hair and pieces of scalp had adhered to the bricks where she'd scraped her head going down. It was assumed she'd slipped on the ice and fallen in; fingernail scratches on the curbing indicated that she'd tried to catch herself and failed.

I'd been in Franklin that day, watching my daughter Sharon roller-skate. We'd just gotten home when the line ring came about Bernice. You can't mistake a line ring: the insistent *zzzt-zzzt-zzzt* goes on until presumably everybody picks up their phone to learn what the emergency is. Half the time the operator announces that school is closed or the Eastern Star meeting is canceled, but often it's real tragedy. It rang on April 17, 1947, the day the tractor turned over on Marston and crushed his chest. That date will never be anything else for me, just as June twelfth will never be anything but the date we were supposed to get married. It rang when Marvin Jobe drowned, when Tom Groner's little gal Lotte burned to death on a haystack, and the morning Audrey and Jim were found in their car poisoned by carbon monoxide. It rang on February 4, 1954, the night Jerry Blake burned to death along with his store. It rang on July 18, 1951, while I sat at home sewing a dress for Sharon's fourth birthday. I lifted the receiver to hear that my sister Anne had been found dead in her car outside the Club 75 and that Frankie Friedland had been shot trying to escape—

Gladys Schmit came into the store with her overshoes flopping, uncoiling a woolen scarf from around her neck. She pulled off her embroidered mittens, remarked how nice it was to see a thaw after three weeks of snow and ice, then with a birdlike jerk of her head she asked:

"Who was that young man with the beard?"

After thirty years of teaching school, Gladys treated the entire community as though they'd never left her fifth and sixth grade room.

"Curt..." I said, and the last name stuck in my throat. "Curt Friedland."

Her eyes went round behind silver-rimmed spectacles. For a moment her lips pursed in a childish disappointment which reminded me that Gladys was, after all, pushing sixty.

"I didn't know he was coming back."

I fingered the ball-point pens in the rack and said nothing. Gladys peered at me with a look of bright interest: "What's he going to do?"

"You'll have to ask him, Gladys. I don't know."

"You knew him, didn't you?"

"He was four years younger than I. You couldn't say I knew him."

"Oh." She was frowning, obviously trying to get in touch with her memory. Then, giving an abrupt jerk of her head, she picked up a loaf of bread and brought it to the counter. "He was the youngest of the four, I remember now. His brothers were so rowdy and athletic. Nobody thought there was brains in the family until they brought that intelligence test in, and Curt made the highest score in the state. People were amazed, he was always so shy and polite...."

I thought: Gladys, *are we talking about the same one?* I remembered seeing Curt fight a larger boy on the playground; Curt had seemed to back away, trying to flee in panic, and my heart had gone out to the kid because I thought he needed help. He backed against the barbed-wire fence which ran between the playground and a cornfield; the other boy lunged, flailing his arms. Curt sidestepped abruptly and the boy crashed into the fence. Curt turned and began hammering with his small fists; when the other boy tried to defend himself he ripped his arms on the sharp barbs. The other boy had finally run away crying. with blood streaming from the gashes on his arms and dripping off his fingers. He'd had twenty stitches taken and Curt hadn't a bruise. The boy's parents had wanted Curt punished, but there was nothing to he done; Curt hadn't cut the boy, the boy had cut himself. Only those of us watching realized that Curt had deliberately maneuvered the boy into the fence. I'd stopped feeling sorry for Curt at that moment; from then on I'd pitied those who were deceived by his quiet manner.

Gladys was telling how, as alumni secretary, she'd kept Curt's address up-to-date in order to send him invitations to the alumni banquet. In five years she'd traced him around the world: "Germany, France, Italy, Tangier, Morocco, Mexico. Japan. Hong Kong. Hawaii. Haiti. Costa Rica. I sent him questionnaires for the school paper and he filled in occupations like opium peddler, beachcomber, ship's cook, taxi driver, things like that. I was so relieved when he settled down and got a college degree, then got a job with that research firm. When he started his own firm I thought, Well *finally* one of the Friedlands will amount to something. Then six months ago his questionnaire came back from the West Indies. He'd listed his occupation as fisherman. Now he's here." She pulled on her mittens and tucked the bread under her arm. "Well, Curtis wasn't like his brothers. He won't cause trouble."

She went out with her overshoes flopping and I thought, No, he won't unless he wants to, but I think he wants to....

I didn't mention him to my husband that night; I didn't want to get involved with Curt Friedland, even to the extent of talking about him.

The next day I stood at the window of the store and saw Curt Friedland drive by in an old car, throwing off a pinwheel of dirty slush which stuck to the parked cars. My husband followed in his pickup with his dark-furred arm out the window. He saw me and drew a circle in the air with his finger, then pointed in the direction Curt was going. That meant he was going to show some property and wouldn't be home for dinner. Lou had at least ten places listed but I was sure which one it was: the old Friedland place back on Brush Creek, vacant since the elder Friedlands had moved near Jeff City so they could visit Frankie on weekends.

We would become involved with Curt, I could see that. I wanted to tell Lou, don't sell to that man, but it wouldn't make any difference. Lou would go on selling, buying, dealing, making money regardless of what I did. Regardless of what *he* did, even; Lou was like a snowball rolling downhill which picks up a gob here and a gob there and suddenly you find it's enormous and what can you do with it all... ?

A hubbub down the street announced the school's morning recess. Sharon came in like a whirlwind of thick black hair and gave me a hard sell about having supper with Sue before the basketball game. She said her current boy friend would drive her home afterward; I put forth a token resistance but in the end I relented and off she went, a darkly exotic fifteen-year-old image of her father. A group of boys in a parked car called out an invitation, and I felt a tingle of pride at the way she handled it—no kittenish play-anger, just a cool no-thank-you. I thought of my own self-conscious adolescence; I could see myself in worn shoes getting off the school bus from Brush Creek and walking that long fifty yards to the schoolhouse door. My stomach would knot when I saw the cluster of boys around the foot-scraper: I couldn't ignore their taunts. I felt I had to insult them in return or else pick up a handful of rocks and let fly as I passed. Well, Sharon had the advantage of what passed locally for wealth. I doubted that she'd have gone through the same ordeal even without it, having inherited her father's... what? Self-centered poise? Selfishness? Not a kind word at all....

A curious feeling of discontent crept through my mind. I started to add up the tickets on the morning deliveries but my attention dwindled away. A car passed with the sound of fat frying in a skillet and I saw that it was Bill Struble coming back from the depot. Life goes on, I thought. Bill still met the trains, but he'd been dazed and withdrawn since his wife's accident. Nobody knew him well and if he had any suspicions about his wife's death he wasn't saying anything. He'd locked up his house and taken a room in own; he'd put his place up for sale and asked for a transfer, so it was clear he had no love for the city of Sherman.

Across the street I saw that the old men had moved from the inside of the pool hall to the slatted bench outside. Harbinger of spring.... Old watery eyes trailing the young girls drifting in threes and fours toward the schoolhouse. Twenty years ago I'd made the same walk; there'd been different faces but the same ragged Mackinaws, same speckled hands on gnarled canes, blue smoke puffing up from corncob pipes. The town didn't change much; it dried up and got smaller, and each Saturday night a few less people came to town. When I was young, Saturday night had brought clusters of men in faded overalls, faces sunburned up to the middle of their foreheads, dead-white from there to the hairline where their hats had held off the sun. Women in wrinkled stockings lined the benches before the stores, talking in tired murmurs while babies fed from white breasts spilled out through flowered print dresses. There were brawls in the alley behind Cott's dance hall (closed during the war and never reopened) and once there was a shooting. (The date was July 4, 1936, a year of drought and despair and desperate gaiety, free government flour with Dad on the WPA and brother in the CCC. I was sitting on the fender of our old Model-A feeling sick because I'd just seen a boy stick a firecracker in a toad's mouth and light it. I saw the man running up the street with the sheriff behind him. Sheriff Wade was young then but heavy; he was falling behind. Then his forty-five roared twice and echoes thundered through the summer night. The locusts stopped chirring and the dogs slopped barking. In the sudden hush the running man spread his arms in a swan dive and fell on his face. He kicked while blood gushed from his month. It was the first time I'd ever seen a man die, and I realized that in death man has no more dignity than a dog kicked by a mule. The dead man had left another man in the alley behind Cott's with his stomach slashed open. The man got his stomach sewed up and was talking and smoking a cigaret an hour later. But the dead man was a dead-broke drifter and nobody grieved.)

That was the depression in Sherman. During the war boys in khaki staggered in the street and fought in the alley; afterward they loafed around wearing ruptured ducks and pieces of old uniforms. When their unemployment payments ran out, they drifted to Kansas City to pack meat or to California to build airplanes. Sometimes when their parents die they come back and try to farm the old place, but they usually sell out and Lou has another listing.

That night I asked Lou over supper: "Sell anything?"

"Umm... not yet."

Lou had a private rule never to discuss a transaction until it was finished, the deed signed and the money deposited. There was no point in trying to discuss Curt with him even if I'd wanted to; he'd have turned cagey and talked around the subject. When it comes to business, Lou seems to forget I'm his wife.

But the next day I knew the deal had gone through and that Cart

Friedland was settling in Sherman. His wife came into the store just before noon. I knew it had to be her; we don't get two unrelated strangers in a single week. She wore no makeup. Her short, thick-curled hair spilled from the front of her white woolen cap like glossy purple grapes. Her tanned face was narrow; her eyes large and hazel, with an element of softness. They made her look surprised and bewildered, and I wanted to help her.

But I didn't. I watched her push her cart around the store picking up the things you need to restock a house: condiments, spices, flour and canned staples. She wore a preoccupied, totally introverted air, as though unaware that she had the attention of everyone in the store. The bread man had dropped two loaves trying to stack bread and watch her at the same time; the candy man had broken off his discussion with me and was peering over the shelves at her. She wore a hip-length mink jacket and tight toreador pants which revealed the abrupt beginning curve of her buttocks below the jacket. She wore the fur as though it were something to keep her warm; a combination of the elegant and shoddy (her ski boots, for example, were scuffed and muddy) made her look as though she'd grown up in wealth and no longer noticed it.

Gladys Schmit must have been watching the store; she came in five minutes later and examined the shelves of pickles. Gladys didn't eat pickles, but that's where Curt's wife was. I heard Gladys ask: "Aren't you Curtis Friedland's wife?"

The girl paused as though thinking it over, then said: "Yes. I'm Gabrielle."

Gladys launched her schoolmarm's interrogation about Gabrielle's career, her husband, and her plans. Gabrielle dodged none of the questions, but answered them in a way which told Gladys only what she knew already: that they'd sold their business in Chicago, spent a few months in the Caribbean, then come here. Gladys attempted to trade confidences; she told about having Curt in school, and how intelligent he was...

"...But so shy and unsure of himself. I used to tell him, go ahead, don't doubt yourself, but he never..."

The girl was not interested. Having defined the old woman's relationship to her husband and decided there was nothing she wanted, she answered in polite monosyllables until Gladys ran down and departed. Then she wheeled her cart to the counter and said to me:

"It seemed like she was talking about someone else. He isn't like that."

She'd done nothing to me except marry into the Friedlands, but I'm really not an outgoing type; I'm narrow and suspicious and mean-tempered, like most Brushcreekers. I busied myself in ringing up her purchases. "People change," I said.

She gave a vague lost smile. "They don't, really."

I ripped off the long ribbon of tape and laid it before her. While I was boxing her purchases, the guilt crept in. After all, she was a stranger in our xenophobic little village and it was pointless to be rude to her. I told her who I was and asked if she'd like to visit some afternoon.

She laid a fifty-dollar bill on the counter and gave me an unblinking look: "Does this include Curt?"

So... she wouldn't let me off the book. I slightly admired her honesty. "I saw him earlier. Didn't he tell you?"

"Yes. He said you'd changed. You used to be friends."

My face felt hot. "It was a long time ago."

"Yesterday," she said. "It all happened yesterday."

I frowned at her. "What do you mean?"

"I've got a man," she said, "who had it all in his hands. Success. Then he threw it away. Why? Because he skipped a turn. He says life is a downhill slalom and if you miss a run the rest of the run doesn't count. No matter how good it is. He thinks he could have saved Frankie if he'd been here, but the air force doesn't give emergency furloughs for murder trials."

I was shocked at the change in her. Instead of a lost, bewildered girl, I was suddenly faced by a passionate, self-assured woman; eyes blazing, coat thrown back and hands on hips, small breasts thrust against a white cashmere sweater. She had a raw physical appeal, a certain savage sexuality which I'd missed the first time.

I lowered my eyes and started counting out her change. "You think Frankie's innocent?"

"I don't question my husband's convictions."

"And he thinks so?"

"Curt doesn't question Frankie's word." She smiled and put the change in her purse. "We all have our little dogmas, don't we?"

I knew what she meant, and I wanted to tell her that I'd wondered about Frankie's guilt—even doubted it—but that I was neither detective nor lawyer... and no matter what happened Anne would remain in her grave...

But I said nothing, and she turned and walked away. I started to call that she'd left her groceries when I saw her speak to a man who'd been leaning against the building. He came in and I saw that it was Guilford Sisk, about six-feet-four of good-natured male with bony wrists hanging from the sleeves of a red and black Mackinaw. He wore his woolen cap pushed off his forehead so the earflaps rested on his ears. He grinned at me self-consciously and jerked his head toward the groceries.

"Those belong to Missus Friedland?"

I nodded. "Are you working for her, Gil?"

"That wouldn't be work," he said with a wink. "No, working for Curt, helping him fix up the old house. It's pretty shot."

That puzzled me, because Gil wasn't one of the men who generally hired out his labor. On the contrary, Gil was one of the biggest landowners in the county. His great-grandfather had come out from Ohio with a Union Army land grant for most of the choice bottomland around Sherman. Gil's grand-father had gradually acquired the rest of it, and there was nothing for their descendants to do but enjoy themselves while the land increased in value. Gil was the last remaining member of the family. He hadn't married; he told me once that he was only interested in one woman and that was me. Yet he'd never proposed in a way that I could take seriously. I enjoyed talk-ing to him because he was intelligent and well-educated; now and then he'd bring up something I'd never heard of, then he'd explain it—not with exasperated patience, as though he were instructing a child, as Lou often did—but with enthusiasm, as though he was as interested in it as I was. I sometimes got the feeling that Gil and I were expatriates in a foreign land, forced together because we could talk only among ourselves. Lou was in-telligent too, but he didn't get along with Gil. Our home place was sur-rounded by Gil's land; Lou wanted to branch out and Gil wouldn't sell. That could have been the reason for the coolness between them, or it could have been me. Gil had never made a pass at me which I could definitely identify, and I had never given him any openings. (I don't think a woman ever gets an offer she doesn't invite, unless it's from a boob, a stranger, a nut who's showing off for friends, or a drunk. No reasonably intelligent man is going to approach a woman without encouragement, and I'd never given it to Gil.) It's true that he had a bad reputation... he'd grown up with fast cars and girls who never said no. Even now he had no respect for the institution of marriage. "A married man's got to uphold the sacred bond of matrimony," he told me once. "He doesn't want someone plowing his own field while he's plowing another' s. Me, what have I got to lose?" But if there'd been a spark waiting to flame up we'd both have known it by now. Nothing could sneak up and surprise us; we'd talked too long and too frankly. He didn't need me, anyway; when he wanted that kind of amuse-ment he'd go down to Kaycee or up to Chicago and bring back a girl to stay a few weeks in his huge three-story brick mansion. He didn't live there, he merely camped in one or the other of its thirty-eight rooms. When he got tired of the woman he sent her home, then plunged into an orgy of work. You'd see him out working on his land, digging post holes, pitching hay and cutting wood, no different than any of his farm hands. He was a strange and rootless man, and despite all our profound conversations, I had the feeling I'd only skated on the surface of his character.

I watched him shoulder the box and I asked: "What's your game now, Gil?"

"With her?" He shook his head soberly. "No game. The kid doesn't know how to play." He stuck a cigaret in his mouth and struck a kitchen match on his thumb. He was full of such overdone yokel mannerisms. "Neither one of them knows how to play, Velda. You might keep that in mind when you're around Curt."

My face grew warm, but I didn't rise to his bait. "Well... what are they doing here?"

He shrugged. "We'll see, Velda. Be patient."

I watched him walk out, and then it struck me. Gil had been Frankie Friedland's best friend. He'd also known Anne not in a romantic sense, but as a member of her group.

And he'd been unable to prove where he was the night Anne was killed.

I felt as though a dismal fog were settling slowly over the community. I didn't want to think about it. I started unpacking soup cans and stacking them in a pyramid.

I was still at it when Ethel reported for work. She was a small erect woman with a hyperthyroid bulge in her eyes. Her husband had once owned the store, but his car had stalled on a rural railroad crossing and he hadn't gotten out in time. She'd sold the store to Louis, but then she'd found time heavy on her hands and come to work for me. Usually she relieved me at one and closed up at six, but today she had something to tell me which wouldn't wait. She'd spent the morning with a sister who worked in the traffic bureau in the county seat of Franklin. The sister had a friend in charge of circuit court records, and guess who had come in that morning and bought a transcript of the Friedland trial....

"Curt Friedland," I said.

Ethel blinked at me, her eyes magnified by thick-lensed spectacles. "How'd you know?"

"The town is in suspended animation. Nothing moves, only Curt Friedland."

"Well... " Ethel's tone was deflated. "He also asked for the coroner's report on Bernice Struble, but that wasn't available. You know what they say?"

"Who says?" I asked.

A wave of her hand included the entire community. "They say he's trying to clear his brother."

I looked up at Ethel, suddenly hating the community for its inability to mind its own business.

"Who says, Ethel?"

"Everybody. And you know what else they say?"

"For God's sake, don't dribble it out. *Say it!*"

The pyramid collapsed, and I walked off and left the cans rolling. As I opened the door to my cubbyhole office, she called after me:

"They say Bernice was probably murdered!"

I slammed the door and lit a cigaret. I tried to work on the charge account ledger, but I couldn't get interested in who owed us money. We had enough money already. I pulled on my cloth coat and walked out. I said good-by to Ethel but she didn't answer. Well, she'd survive the blow.

Driving east in the station wagon, I found myself humming a song under my breath: *Oh-oh, trouble's back in town.* I could only remember one line, but it seemed to fit....

I drove north on the gravel, then turned right and passed beneath a stone archway. The open wrought-iron gates—initialed LB for Louis Bayrd—made me feel as though I were entering a cemetery. I drove up the curving lane which Lou had paved and bordered with evergreens. He'd made his aunt's old farm look like a country estate; white fences enclosed sloping pastures; chunky Herefords grazed amid a shrinking patchwork of snow; a sorrel mare and a black gelding trotted with the car along an old-fashioned rail fence. Towering elms and red oaks flanked a white neo-colonial house and a five-acre lawn sloped down to a pint-sized lake stocked with swans and bluegills. Lou had put up a diving board and planted shrubbery, then had grumbled because Sharon and I didn't use it more. So we'd used it fiercely for a month and Lou had happily gone on to something else: converted the old farmhouse into a workshop, jammed it to the roof with power tools and built a power cruiser. Now the boat squatted on its trailer gathering dust, waiting for summer and sunshine on Lake Pillybay. We'd probably use it two or three times. When did Lou enjoy himself? What drove him? I couldn't answer because he never sat still long enough for me to see him.

The kitchen was polished brick and sparkling copper. I washed the breakfast dishes, opened a can of pork and beans and ate, washing it down with milk. I brewed coffee and drank it with a slow cigaret, feeling the silence of the huge empty house seep into my body. I liked the lonely afternoons at home. Evenings there was Lou, mornings the store, but in the afternoons I led my own life.

I washed the dishes and debated whether to take a bath or a shower. I decided against a bath; it made me lazy and sexual, like a cat licking itself in the sun. Today I needed movement. I showered under water blended to give just a tingle of coolness. I dried myself before the heating vent, letting the warm air caress my skin. I pulled on blue jeans and a sweatshirt and walked down to the pasture. I pumped water for the horses and let them nibble sugar lumps out of my palms. I noticed that the gelding had gotten fat during the cold spell. I took the hackamore off the windmill and pulled it over his head. I rode him bareback, raising my face to the wind and feeling his great muscles roll between my thighs. After a half hour I slid off and removed the hackamore. I could feel the warmth and dampness of perspiration against my thighs. I took another shower and went into the studio Lou had built for me. I pulled the drapes and filled the room with purple twilight. I sat down at the piano and played songs I knew by heart. My fingers moved without direction; my thoughts dwindled away....

Lou came home around eleven.

I lay with my light off, pretending sleep, listening to the sounds as he prepared for bed: slap of wallet on the dresser... jingle of keys, change... *clump-clump* of shoes... clatter of hangers as he hung up his clothes. I visualized him: deceptively small and built like a chunk of stovewood, black hair swirling about his thighs and curling up from his chest in great tufts. Lou was humming. He always did when he performed some task which didn't fully occupy his mind. I strained my ears and caught the tune: *Oh-oh, trouble's bank in town.* I was shocked to realize I'd become so closely linked to this man that Curt's arrival would trigger the same train of thought.

Before he got into his bed, he set the controls of the electric eye which bracketed the drive. When a car passed through the gate, the beam would be broken and the drive floodlighted. Lou wasn't nervous about burglars; he just did it for amusement, like the shop and the boat. I'd asked him before not to turn it on when Sharon had a date, but he did it anyway.

I heard him get into the bed across from mine and light a cigaret, then he said:

"Curt Friedland bought his dad's old place."

There. How the hell did he know I was awake? I sat up and lit a cigaret. I saw the ashtray heaped full of butts and realized how he'd known. Lou never missed the little things....

"Why?" I asked. I was surprised at the coldness of my voice.

"He was born there."

"So were his brothers. They haven't come back."

"A man gets lost, he has to return to the starting place to find himself again."

"You think Curt's lost?"

"Who isn't?"

It was one of my husband's non-answers. Ask him if he's cold and if he doesn't want to think about it he says: Who isn't? Ask him if he likes fried chicken, he says: Who doesn't? Then I get hung up trying to think of somebody who doesn't like fried chicken and I forget the original question.

At that point the floodlights came on. Poor Sharon.

I exhaled slowly, trying to keep cool. "I knew a girl who was whipped when her father caught her with a boy. So she went the whole distance every chance she got. She knew she'd be punished anyway."

"What's that got to do with Sharon?"

"Give her a chance for a normal relationship."

"It's normal to sit in a parked car for hours?"

I sighed. "Yes, Lou. It's normal."

He got up and turned off the floodlights, then lay back down. I was surprised at his quick acquiescence until I realized he probably wanted something from me. Maybe he only wanted to talk about the Friedlands; at least he started that way. They seemed to have no money worries, he said; Curt had paid for the place with a ten-thousand-dollar cashier's check on a Chicago bank and deposited the rest. The van had been waiting with their furniture and Lou had helped them move in. "Nothing fancy," said Lou, "just quietly expensive. A few antiques that his wife shepherded along. I think she comes from money. Also two electric typewriters, hi-fi, tape recorder, adding machine, stuff like that. Curt's firm didn't go broke the way some people thought; he was in opinion research, and he suddenly decided be didn't give a damn about other people's opinions. He sold out and went to the islands, goofed around in a native dugout while his wife made shell jewelry. Then he got the idea of coming back to fix up the old place..."

Lou swung his legs off the bed and sat up. "I like the way he does business. No scratching his head, no hemming and hawing. It's either yes or no and it's obviously final either way. He lets his wife run things on the surface. If he doesn't like it she changes it around until he does. She used to manage the field end of the business, door-to-door canvassers, telephone interviewers, mail questionnaires. She's not a brain, but she's sharp as a knife." He smiled vaguely. "Pretty too."

I gave him a narrow look. His face was flushed—probably from drinking—and there was a rare brightness in his eyes, the pinpointed, dazzled look of someone hypnotized. I had a good idea who'd done it.

"You and Curt worked pretty late?"

"Not too. We took off at eleven and went to the Club 75. Goober Sutton and his wife kept staring at Curt and mumbling to each other. I thought Goober was going to call the law when Curt started bugging him."

"I thought your friend was so cool."

"He is. He did it deliberately, to get information."

"Didn't he ever hear of the friendly approach?"

Lou sighed and stretched out on the bed. "The friendly approach elicits platitudes and false cordiality. Your front is undisturbed; you can sit there lying with your teeth showing in a great big smile. On the other hand, if you bug a man, he's liable to get mad. And when he gets mad he tells the truth whether he wants to or not. Not verbally, but by his actions."

"That sounds like a direct quote from Curt."

"I guess it is."

"You think he's pretty smart?"

Lou stood up and walked around the room, his pajamas flapping. "Look, I don't mean he tweaked his nose or anything. Just shook hands and asked if Goober remembered him. Then he looked around and said, 'You've changed things around, haven't you, Goober?' Goober was beginning to stiffen up. 'We've made several changes over the years,' he said. And Curt said, 'That wall, I mean. You didn't have that partition say, twelve years ago, did you?' Goober looked like he had stomach trouble. He said: 'No, we didn't.' And Curt said, 'You've added a lot of lights to your parking lot too. It's bright as day out there. Not much hanky-panky could go on now.' I could see Goober wishing Curt would give him some excuse to go for that lead-filled club he's got under the bar. Finally Curt said: 'Look, I don't want you to think I hold anything against you. I don't. You told the truth as you saw it, what else could you do?' Remember, Goober testified that Frankie got mean and violent when he drank; he upset Frankie's picture of himself as a good-natured, harmless drinker, and it had a lot to do with the verdict. Anyway, Goober looked like a boiled beet. He opened his mouth but Curt said he didn't have to apologize. Goober blurted that he damn well wasn't *about* to apologize; Curt said he certainly didn't blame him, because there was no need to apologize for telling the truth as he saw it. Jesus... I was about to fall out of the booth laughing. That poor goddam Goober was being led along like a pig with a ring in his nose. Finally he got up and said he was closing for the night and we'd have to leave."

"You enjoyed it, did you?"

Lou smiled. "I like the way he screws people up."

"Sounds to me like he's just trying to make trouble, this hero of yours."

Lou pulled aside the covers and slid into his bed. "Not *just* make trouble, Velda."

"You believe he's trying to clear his brother."

"Naturally," said Lou, stifling a yawn.

"Does he have anything new?"

"I don't think so."

"And Bernice? Does he have any evidence of murder?"

"None that I know of."

"Then what—?"

"Listen, you've gone rabbit hunting with your brother?"

"Yes."

"What did he do when the rabbit ran into a brushpile?"

I frowned, trying to remember. "He threw rocks and made a lot of noise, trying to scare him into the open."

Lou nodded. "And if that didn't work he set fire to the brushpile." Lou frowned at the ceiling. "I'm just guessing, you know. I can't read him at all. He smiles when you can't see anything to smile about. Sort of hangs back, watching you. I don't think his wife understands him either. When she talks to somebody, her eyes keep sliding in his direction to see how he's taking it." Lou paused. "An interesting couple. I thought I'd invite them... "

"Lou." A tone of quiet warning.

"His brother did it, Velda. Curt was in Korea."

"I know that." I was speaking around a pain. "Invite anybody you like. Just don't expect me to entertain them."

"You sound like a Brushcreeker."

"Strange. It happens I am."

"So's Curt."

"Then he'll understand exactly how I feel." I rolled over and turned my back. "Good night."

A moment later the canopy of light between our beds disappeared. I tossed in the darkness and cursed the treachery of my own nervous system. All the girlish uncertainty I thought I'd conquered had only been asleep someplace. Curt's return had brought it popping out like some foolish jack-in-the-box grinning its floppy head at me. I knew that Curt had trapped Lou in a net of curiosity, and I was determined not to he caught the same way. I also saw that Lou didn't care whether he was trapped or not, and I was afraid I wouldn't care either—

Oh hell, let's face it. Curt was too smart, and my little boat couldn't stand much rocking. Give me credit for knowing that much.

CHAPTER TWO

I was standing at the store window next morning when Gabrielle strolled through the park with Sandra Matthews. Sandy was a Brush Creek girl whom the boys used to pick up around midnight and take home the long way. Poor Sandy had the illusion that this was what they meant when they talked about popularity. She'd been in the Club 75 with Frankie the night of Anne's murder, and she'd testified at the trial.

I could picture the courtroom at Franklin; I could hear the muffled coughs and hushed whispers. I smelled musty paper and ancient varnish and I saw Sandy on the stand, so serious that she looked mournful. She wore a navy-blue suit and black patent-leather pumps, the same outfit she'd worn to Anne's funeral. She testified that Frankie had drunk perhaps a half dozen beers and sampled a friend's bottle of bourbon. When the prosecutor asked if Frankie was drunk, Frankie's lawyer objected that Sandy wasn't qualified to judge drunkenness. The judge sustained the objection, and the prosecutor went on to ask what happened when Frankie was told that Anne was waiting in the car:

Sandy: *Well, I was bugged. I mean, he was my date, after all. I asked him why he didn't go out and finish with her for good. I didn't mean—*

Prosecutor: *You meant he should stop seeing her?*

That's what I meant.

What did Frankie say?

For me to worry about myself. He'd take care of Anne.

What do you think he meant?

The defense objected that Sandy's opinions were irrelevant, and the judge sustained it. In cross-examination, Sandy admitted that to the best of her knowledge Frankie and Anne were on intimate terms and hadn't quarreled.

Since the trial, Sandy had acquired a husband named George Bennett, four children, and fifty pounds of fat which trembled as she walked. She still talked about the murder and hinted that she hadn't told all she knew, but nobody listened to her any more.

I watched the two of them together: slim Gabrielle and dumpy, dowdy Sandy with a baby on her hip, haunches rolling, like a plow horse mistakenly teamed with a show horse. The pair sat on a bench in the sun; Sandy dumped a large gray breast from her dress, shoved it into the baby's mouth, covered it with her sweater, and talked. I knew she was babbling about the murder because that's all she ever talked about....

A blue Mercury rolled past with the words FRANKLIN COUNTY SHERIFF painted on its door. It parked in front of the building where Lou had his hardware store and real estate office. Sheriff Glen Wade went in wearing his .38 in a button-down holster on his belt. The visit wasn't unusual; Lou was a leading citizen and president of the Lions Club; it was an election year and Lou was supporting the sheriff. Still, I had a feeling it concerned Curt Friedland. I'd seen Lou leave town a half hour before with a load of doorframes and roofing—destined for Curt's house, I was sure— so I wasn't surprised when the sheriff came into the store.

"Hello, Velda," he said. "Know where I could find Lou?"

"I sure don't, Sheriff." The lie surprised me; I thought I'd outgrown the Brushcreeker's inborn antagonism toward the law.

The sheriff made a show of examining the display of stainless-steel razor blades. It had been over twenty-five years since I'd watched him kill the man in the street, but I could never forget that he wore death on his hip. He couldn't have been more than thirty then; even now he retained the blunt, beefy good looks of an aging athlete who keeps in shape.

Finally he spoke in a blurred baritone: "I hear Lou sold the old Friedland place."

The sheriff had small gray eyes; you looked in and it left you sort of empty, as though you'd failed to locate a person inside.

I forced down an impulse to lie. "So he said."

"The boy bought it outright, they say."

"That's what Lou says."

The sheriff pulled at his belt and shifted his weight to the other foot. "I don't get over to this end of the county much. Don't need to these days. Brush Creek's kind of farmed out and the troublemakers have left. People like your husband keep things in line. But a sheriff isn't worth his salt if he can't smell trouble in the wind, isn't that right?"

"That's right, Sheriff."

The sheriff looked relieved. "What I was wondering, have you heard any rumors that might concern law enforcement?"

Something seemed to rip the words out of my mouth. "I heard that Bernice Struble was murdered."

The sheriff looked pained. "Now, Velda, you know that ain't true."

I shrugged and said nothing, watching his face turn hard and heavy. I could almost see his massive strength bunching beneath his light-blue gabardine jacket. Finally he gave a short decisive nod.

"Think I'd better check up on that rumor. See you later, Velda."

I watched him get in his car and drive off toward Franklin. That puzzled me because I'd gotten the idea he was going after Curt. Then I remembered that he never went into the Nation alone, just as city policemen never patrolled tough neighborhoods alone. He'd gone to get his deputy.

I glanced over in the park. Gaby and Sandy were gone. I couldn't see Curt's car anywhere around the square. I tried to add up the tickets on the morning deliveries, but I couldn't make sense out of the numbers. I knew what was wrong; my past kept jumping up and hitting me in the face. I picked up the phone and called Ethel: "Can you come in and take over? I've got to rush out of town."

The streaked old frame house sat on a barren hill in the bowels of the Nation. A single pine tree stood beside the house, its trunk naked except for a tuft of green at the top. The Friedland boys had always kept 'coon hounds chained to the tree; they'd also had stretching frames for curing muskrat and mink pelts, and a small graveyard of junked cars and wrecked motorcycles. For ten years the sightless windows had overlooked gullied slopes which resembled the ribs of a starving dog.

Now the house had the bustling disorder of a mining camp. A telephone company truck was parked on the road, and men were stringing wire toward the house. Heine Wentz' drilling rig squatted half-way up the slope beside a pyramid of fresh yellow clay. I didn't see Lou's pickup nor Curt's old car; apparently Gaby hadn't yet returned. I recognized Gil Sisk's hulking figure on the roof and waved; he spat out a handful of nails and called down:

"Lou went to Connersville for plumbing fixtures."

I nodded. Connersville was the nearest large city, forty miles away. "Where's Curt?"

Gil's face spread in a teasing grin. "What you want him for?"

My face felt hot. "It's serious, Gil. Where is he?"

Gil silently pointed his hammer across a flat stretch of ground behind the house. I saw Curt's back outlined against the sky; broad and tan and bare to the waist, with a quiver of arrows across it. Far ahead of him stood an archery target.

I made my way over the rocky ground. A light breeze caressed my face, warm until the sun went behind a fleck of cloud, then sharp with the bite of winter.

"You're rushing the season," I said as I walked up behind him. "It isn't that warm."

He turned, and I was surprised to see that he'd shaved off the beard. His face was composed of straight lines coming together in perfect angles, so smooth that I looked hard for a flaw. There was something unnaturally clean and hard about his face; you couldn't say about him: Here's a thoughtful man, or a sad and morose man. He seemed... blank, like someone in a waiting room. I felt an urge to see some emotion in the face, and to know that I'd caused it myself. Anything would have served, even hatred or disgust.

But he looked at me without change of expression and turned back.

With a single smooth movement, he took an arrow from the quiver and fitted it to the bowstring.

"I've still got the West Indian sun in my system. The cold hasn't touched me yet."

I felt like a bug which had been seized, stuck under a microscope, and set aside. I forced down my annoyance, remembering that I'd been to blame for our awkward reunion yesterday. It was up to me to erase that beginning.

"I... like you better without the beard."

"It was part of my beachcomber costume." A vague smile tugged at his lips, as though he were laughing at himself. "Now I'm on another masquerade."

We were still stalking on the surface. I felt impatient to make contact, to get beneath his shield. I watched his muscles knot as he slowly drew back the bowstring. A dew of sweat shone on his forehead, but his features were composed. Suddenly all his muscles went slack. Zzzzp! The arrow disappeared; I saw it reappear a second later in the second ring out from the bull's-eye.

"I never saw anyone shoot like that."

"It's the Zen method," he said, drawing another arrow from the quiver. "You're supposed to let the release of the arrow come as a total surprise. You aren't supposed to think."

ZzzzP! A second arrow quivered in the edge of the bull's-eye.

"Pretty good," I said. "Zen is a kind of Buddhism, isn't it, like yoga?"

He nodded.

"You sit with your feet in your lap?"

He smiled, an exasperating controlled flicker at the corner of his mouth which made me want to say: For God's sake, let it go, laugh a little.

"Sometimes," he said. "But only when I feel like it."

Mysticism. I don't know why it made me wistful. That was one of the trails I'd never taken and I sort of wished I had....

He turned, and I saw that I'd somehow broken through. His frozen, guarded look was gone. "If you'd like to try, I'll get you Gaby's bow. It's got a lighter pull."

"Not now," I said. "I came to tell you to expect a visit from the sheriff."

He nodded. "I was already expecting it."

I felt disappointed. "Why?"

He fitted another arrow into the bow. "The sheriff has an opponent for office, a bright ex-marine just out of college. I met him the other day and made a small campaign contribution. He was interested in the fact that I used to do public opinion surveys; wanted to know what I thought his chances were. I told him I'd check around and try to give him something he could use in his campaign."

"You aren't even trying to get along with Sheriff Wade, are you?"

"Sheriff Wade is a bloated bag of ego. All he cares is that everything looks peaceful. The county's like a garbage dump with fresh dirt smoothed over it; underneath it's a seething mass of maggots."

"Oh... not *that* bad."

He gave me a glance of pity. "You've been in it so long you don't even notice."

He turned and sent an arrow into the center of the bull's eye. I watched him slide the quiver off his shoulder and unstring the bow, and I tried to understand my own vague feeling that he was right about Sheriff Wade—and the county too.

He picked his sweatshirt off the ground and pulled it over his head. "Actually," he said, "there was never any question of getting along with the sheriff. We were opposed by the nature of things. My tie-in with the opposition is a form of insurance. If the sheriff tries to give me the roust I go straight to the other guy, who'll spread it all over the country. If the sheriff's smart he'll handle me easy."

I looked at Curt curiously. "You always figure things to the fourth decimal point?"

He shrugged. "Sometimes, Velda. I can't help using what I know to control my environment. Sheriff Wade happens to be part of my environment. I do what I can."

We were walking toward the house when I said: "You manage to get a lot of free labor; my husband, Gil Sisk..."

"Tom Sawyer and the fence. They want to find out what I'm doing here."

"What are you doing here?"

He looked at me. "Your husband trusts you, doesn't he?"

It was a statement, not a question. I don't know why, but I suddenly felt stodgy and middle-aged. "He has no reason not to."

Curt nodded. "I suppose he'd understand if we went for a ride—-in your car."

"Of course," I said quickly.

Not until we were on the road, and he'd directed me toward Lake Pillybay, did I wonder: Would I have gone it he'd put it differently? I decided I probably would have; I had nothing better to do.

I drove silently, leaving the steep marginal farmlands behind, ascending slowly along the ridge. Snow lay white beneath naked trees on the slopes below. Curt lit a cigaret and put it between my lips. I accepted without surprise until I realized I'd have resented the intimacy from another man. I understood that I shared something with Curt that I'd never shared with Lou: we had less need for talk; a glance or a word held special meanings which we both understood. It all had something to do with growing up on a rocky farm during a depression....

"Why did you come back?" I asked.

He waved his hand. "This is where it all happened, the first sixteen years of my life. Compared to what the last sixteen have been... dull, repetitive. This is where everything happened first." He pointed to a stream far below. "There, for example..." He broke off with a laugh.

"There what? Don't laugh in your beard. You don't have it any more."

"My first lesson in sex."

"Oh?" My stomach went curiously tight. "With whom?"

"Sandy Matthews."

I felt a vague disappointment. "You didn't pick a very high-class teacher."

"No..." Then he frowned. "I'm not sure, though. I was fourteen, Sandy was three years older. She asked me, and I was trapped by pride. I couldn't say no, and I couldn't admit that I'd never done it before. She took me to an old barn we used to have; she acted so funny I got suspicious. I looked up and saw eyes peering in. My brothers had set the whole deal up. I was fighting mad. I tore out of there and was going to beat up the whole crew, but they ran away. Then I went back and I was going to beat up Sandy too. I found her crying, ashamed. She'd been trapped by a dare. We went for a walk and wound up in the ravine, swimming nude. It really happened then... natural and innocent. I was in love with her for several months." He grunted and pulled out his pipe. "It was... sad to see her again. I wanted to talk to her, but she had only one thing on her mind; she wanted to relive that incident by the stream. It couldn't happen, but she wasn't capable of knowing that. She had youth then; freshness and a kind of innocence. That's all she had, and she lost it." He gave me an oblique look as he lit his pipe. "Something happens to people here. Their bodies look healthy, but the minds inside are dead, sluggish and slow, like cold porridge. What does it, Velda?"

I set my jaws and kept my eyes on the narrow gravel road. He was working up to something, and I had an idea it concerned me.

"Remember after the fight, when the boy got tangled in the fence, you said that ten years from now I'd be ashamed. What did you mean?"

"I... I don't remember."

"See? You had something then. I remember seeing you get on the school bus in the mornings with your chin held high, looking aloof and cold. But with green fire in your eyes. You'd date older boys and I'd feel like you feel when you see a boob on a magnificent horse. They didn't appreciate what they had." He paused. "You've changed. You've fallen victim to life's leveling process. You go to the store in the mornings and talk with housewives and deliverymen. Your terms become those of Ethel and Gladys and Sandy—"

"Oh, Curt—!"

"In the afternoons you go home and... what? I'll bet you've started a dozen hobbies in the last ten years."

I thought of my sewing machine, my guitar, embroidery, sketchpad, typewriter...

"What are you, a detective?"

"An observer. Things have to fit together. I see certain facets of your character—impatient eye movements and excessive smoking, for example—and I deduce that you're restless and bored."

"Well, deduce something else. You're wrong."

"Okay. The hobbies indicate an active, searching mind. Is that better?"

"I... yes."

"Same thing. Active mind. Unoccupied. Gets bored. See?" He laughed shortly. "It's only a word game. Don't give it a thought. You can stop here."

We'd reached the point where the road passed the summit of Bald Knob, highest point in the county. Ahead it descended into Lake Pillybay. I pulled onto the shoulder and Curt got out.

"Want to walk up to the top?"

I gripped the wheel and shook my head. "Curt, you're still playing games with me. You said not to worry, but you didn't mean it. I'm supposed to worry. I'm supposed to feel desperately bored, I'm supposed to say: What can I do, Curt? And then you'll say, Well, you can help me solve this little murder...."

He smiled faintly. "No, just think about it. You've had it buried twelve years, Velda. Think of Frankie. Could he have done it?"

I watched him walk up the hill and I thought about Frankie. He was the second youngest of the four boys, next to Curt. He was also the craziest. He had a strong jaw and curly auburn hair which grew thick and wild. I used to feel about him the way I'd felt about Curt the morning before: this man doesn't care; he's on an emotional roller-coaster, he makes me edgy and nervous, the way I get around strange animals. My image of him is of running and shouting, and something to do with violence... a powerful force unbottled—quite the opposite of Curt, who left an impression of steely control. Frankie was violent, yes, but I never thought he was cruel. I've seen him tear a beer joint apart with a whoop and a holler, but he never stopped laughing. Marston and I were parked along the highway late one night when Frankie roared by on his cycle. He must have been going a hundred and twenty; he was just a blur. A moment later another blurred shape roared by. It was Curt. He was barely in his teens and he followed his brother everywhere. I was afraid for Curt, because I figured Frankie would kill them both....

Frankie went with my sister Anne all through high school. She was prettier than I: big hazel eyes and black hair glinting with blue highlights. She had a sleek windblown look which made you think of the girls they put on hood ornaments. During the war Frankie became a flier and was lost over Germany. They'd planned to get married after he came back, not knowing they should have done it before. My dad was to blame for what happened next; the baby became obvious and we'd been told to presume Frankie dead. Dad told Anne to get a husband and she picked Johnny Drew, a reckless kid who'd been discharged from the marines after getting malaria in the Pacific. For six months afterward he sauntered around town in his dress uniform.

I drew my impression from that: an egocentric fathead who'd carried his bluff this far and run out of gas. I was right, but I got no joy out of it. The baby was stillborn, and instead of getting a sensible divorce, Anne went to hell. If Frankie had come back... but none of the Friedlands came back. The oldest, a Navy frogman, was killed at Eniwetok. The second oldest survived the war as a paratrooper, married a French girl, and settled down in Algeria. After Frankie's release from prison camp he flew for oil companies in Arabia and South America. Around 1948 he went to Alaska and started a flying service for hunters and prospectors. Curt quit school and joined him; started flying at sixteen. Sherman was dull without the Friedlands, but in a sense they were still with us. Anne had become a lovely whore. Every family seems to have one member who goes to hell; I remember Anne during those five years as a dull ache in the heart. She never acquired the bloated, baggy look of a honky-tonk queen—which is the usual way for a girl to go to hell in this part of the country—but she was working on it. She made her home in the Club 75, a rambling roadhouse near Lake Pillybay where tourists and Brushcreekers fought and played together. Know that it was an after-hours' place and you've got the scene: booze-red faces and thick smoke; neckties and denim shirts and black leather jackets jostling together; blood and broken bottles in the parking lot; teenagers getting stoned in the parked cars on booze carried out by older cronies; the sound of retching, the muffled thump of thrashing bodies in back seats and the *squee-squee-squee* of car springs; women with dresses up squatting carelessly between parked cars; men's voices thick with guttural rage and a woman's strident screech: *You suvvabitch I'll go home with whoever I damn please—!*

Queen Anne held court in a knotty-pine booth next to the bar, selecting her escorts with the unpredictability of a royal whim, letting them understand there was nothing in her of permanence or love...

Then came Korea, and Curt went over to fly jets. A year later Frankie drifted home to sweat out the war, saying he couldn't run his business without Curt, since only Curt knew how to keep books and make a profit. And Frankie took up his strange affair with Anne. They seemed to fight against being together; each night they'd go in separate directions with separate groups; each morning around three a.m. they'd be sitting together in a booth at the Club 75. Neither of them had the sense to wipe the slate clean and start over....

Frankie, meanwhile, was playing baseball with a local league, whooping it up around the district, and jousting with the law. It was part of a Brushcreeker's heritage to have law trouble. Frankie was jailed for a week in St. Joe for throwing two bouncers out of their own dance hall; he drew another week in Omaha for tearing up a nightclub; he drew thirty-days in Franklin County Jail for resisting arrest. (He'd taken Deputy Hoff's guns from him and thrown them in a grader ditch, then kicked the deputy in after them. Nobody blamed Frankie; the deputy was a vicious little brute who wore two ridiculous forty-fives low on his hips. He used to walk into the Club 75 slapping his club in his palm, daring somebody to step out of line. Frankie hadn't been able to resist taunting him, and the deputy had been waiting when he left the club.) A week after Frankie's release he was sitting in the club with Sandy when Gil Sisk said Anne wanted to see him in the car. At the trial, Frankie explained it when he took the stand in his own defense:

I usually met Anne at the club and took her home. I just figured she didn't want to come in for some reason, so I went out. She'd parked in the dark and I didn't see anyone in the car. I opened the door and saw her lying across the seat. I reached in to touch her and something blew up in the back of my head. I don't remember anything after that.

Defense Attorney: You made a statement to the sheriff after your arrest that you could remember nothing that happened the night before. Is that true?

Sure, but it all came back to me later. The bump on the head blacked out my memory.

You weren't drunk?

No, I felt good.

What do you mean, you felt good?

I wasn't mad at anybody. I was having a ball.

In the cross-examination, the prosecutor asked:

Isn't it true that in the past your idea of having a ball had led to violence, fighting, destruction—

Objection, which was sustained. The prosecutor then asked why he'd run when they came to arrest him.

Frankie: Hell, I didn't run. Those bastards came out to the house, got me out of bed, and asked me to come with them. My head was splitting and I had a bloody lump on it. I decided I'd busted up some joint the night before and there'd be a stink. I got in and the sheriff took off into the hills, driving slow, asking me questions about the night before. Deputy Hoff had his gun out and was trying to look tough. Little by little I realized somebody had been killed. I got jumpy. I knew the deputy would set me up if he got a chance. So when we stopped—we'd been riding a couple of hours, and eventually you gotta stop—

Who wanted to stop?

The sheriff was driving. He just stopped. We all got out and stood there, you know, taking care of our own business, and I looked at the trees ahead and thought, well, what the hell? So I took off. Blam! Right in the back. Two days later I woke up in the hospital handcuffed to the bed.

Frankie had been found guilty. His family had gone broke appealing the sentence, but it had stuck. Now Curt wanted to open it up. I couldn't see that he had any chance at all.

I got out and walked toward the summit of Bald Knob. Years ago, somebody had cut off the oak and hickory timber in the hope of growing crops, but rain and wind had stripped away the soil and left only jumbled rocks and boulders. Curt sat on a large boulder, smoking his pipe.

"Safest place in the world," he said as I came up. "A barren hill."

I looked at the terrain dropping off in all directions. To the east a glint of light marked the Sherman watertower; to the west I saw tiny patches of silver which were the coves of Lake Pillybay. I could make out the gray roof of the Club 75, squatting in a patch of yellow gravel.

I sat down on the boulder facing away from him. A breeze whispered across the summit, stirred the dead weeds, and teased up my skirt. It felt like cool fingers lightly caressing my thighs. My nose filled with the masculine smell of his tobacco; my back touched his arm, and I felt the warmth of his body through the sweatshirt. A knot of tension formed deep in the pit of my stomach; he had brought me here for some reason. Why? I wondered, knowing that if he tried anything, I'd resist him to the last breath; bracing for him but at the same time waiting, curious to see what he'd do....

Finally I said: "Why do you say safest?"

He waved his hand. "Visibility. You can see trouble coming for miles."

I stared at him. "Are you that scared?"

He smiled. "That's not a good word. I've just developed certain habits, never walk into a dark room with your hands full, never stand in a lighted widow, never tell all you know...."

"But you used to be so... reckless."

"Yes. Well, that's something I lost."

He looked down at his feet a moment, then gave a short, humorless laugh. "Anyway, I wasn't really. Look there, remember that dive Frankie used to do?"

He pointed his pipe toward the lake. I saw the sparkle of water below a limestone cliff, and the low ledge from which we used to dive. My gaze drifted up... up to the very top of the cliff, nearly seventy feet above the water. I remembered Frankie racing across the plateau and leaping off with the chilling scream of an eagle. His tanned muscular body had plummeted past the gaping boys on the ledge and struck the water like a rock. A moment later another shape soared off the cliff and streaked down like a pale arrow, passing the ledge so closely my heart stopped, then knifing the water with hardly a ripple. That had been Curt, outdoing his brother but doing it so quietly that few people noticed; they were busy watching Frankie splash toward shore.

"I remember Frankie's dive," I said. "I also remember yours."

"Yes but... did you know that Frankie made it the first time at night, in absolute darkness? Hell, he didn't know he could clear that ledge below, he just jumped down into the darkness and hoped. You know what I did? I measured the ledge, and I figured I had to leap out fifteen feet to clear it. I practiced the jump from lower down until I was damn sure I could make it."

"Yours was better," I said. I looked at him and he was smiling. "It was. Really."

He shook his head. "Not for me. I only did what I knew I could do. Frankie threw his fate into the lap of the gods and jumped. When he made it he knew they were on his side. I didn't understand that for a long time. Gaby did, though. We had a little cliff on our island, oh ... twenty-five feet high. Water roared into a narrow crevice below it. Gaby used to stand there and time her dive so she'd catch a swell at its peak, otherwise she'd land in three feet of water. Well, the night I decided to come back here— I'd been getting the county newspaper and they'd just brought the one which reported Bernice Struble's death—we had a terrible argument. She didn't want me to come back. She went off mad and was gone until dark. I was about to search for her when I saw her silhouetted against the sky at the top of the cliff. My heart jumped into my mouth. She'd never jumped at night and I thought: Lord, even if she catches the wave right she could hit a chunk of driftwood. Off she went. I met her as she came out of the water and said if she felt like that I wouldn't go. She said no, but that if I wanted to deliberately risk my life she'd do the same.

"Then it hit me. Coming back here was my own jump into darkness. I wasn't sure I could succeed. I knew I'd bump heads with the law, not to mention becoming a target for the real killer. Thinking about it... I was scared, but I was exhilarated too. I was shoving in all I had. I was taking the big jump and at the bottom I'd find either life... or death. Everything was simple."

I looked at him and saw the excitement shining in his eyes. I understood the look I'd seen earlier, of not caring. He'd taken his fate out of his hands and now he was free. And in a way I envied him....

Walking down to the car I said: "You came all the way back here just because Bernice Struble fell in a well?"

"Yes." He looked at me and laughed abruptly. "You think that's crazy?"

"Well, I... Yes. Damn right I do. Especially when you say it's murder and you don't have a single measly crumb of evidence—!"

"I have a theory, Velda. To test a theory you have to act as though it's true. Then you start stacking up the facts and if your theory doesn't hold them all you throw it out. When Frankie got sent up, I was sure of one thing; there was a killer loose in Sherman. I expected him to strike again, sooner or later, but there were no more murders. That didn't fit what I'd learned about killers... until it occurred to me that he was clever enough to make them all look like accidents. I started checking, but it wasn't until Bernice's death that I had something to work on. It could have been an accident, I'll admit. But I have to assume it's murder in order to test the theory. You understand?"

"No." I stopped at the car and turned. "The trouble is you start with the assumption that Frankie didn't kill... my sister. I don't have that faith, you know. He wasn't my brother."

Curt pulled out his billfold and gave me a folded square of paper. It was a penciled note faded and smeared from much handling. It began *Dear Angelface:* that was the nickname Curt's brothers had used when they teased him.

Yr. idea sounds crazy, just between us kids. A good honest cop is worth ten smart lawyers; once the law gets an armlock on a man they quit looking. I got convicted and that's it; I'd bet my tobacco ration that every speck of evidence that didn't agree with the verdict has been shoved under the rug. But okay, I'll answer your questions and shoot this out past the censors. She was dead when I got there.

You know how they feel. I couldn't have been wrong. I must have got home by instinct after I got hit on the head. I don't remember. I didn't black out from booze; Gil Sisk can tell you I wasn't drunk, and you know how I always remembered everything, even when I was totally paralyzed from drinking. So what happened to the knife the killer used? The sheriff never found it, and it's rusted away by now. So damn much of this evidence is cold, cold. One thing to look into: Anne was playing some guy for money. I told her once that I'd go back north if I laid my hands on a bundle, and she asked if I'd take her with me. Half shot, I said sure. Maybe I would've too. Anyway, she visited me in the can while I was sweating out my thirty days and asked me when I could leave, because she thought she could raise about five thou. I said, anytime baby. Could be she had it the night she got killed; did the sheriff find any money on her? Strap that fat-assed son-of-a-bitch down and apply a pair of wire stretchers to his you-know-what. I don't think he knows who killed her, but he knows damn well I didn't. Sandy Matthews might give you something. She said once that Anne should be satisfied with the man she had and not bother me.

She wasn't talking about Johnny Drew, since who'd be satisfied with him? If I think of anything else I'll shoot it out to you, but I'm not holding my breath, buddy-o. Some birds here plan on sprouting wings and they want me in the covey. They'll wait six months, so that's how long you've got. After that I'm out of the game, win or lose. *Buena Suerte*, Angelface.

I gave him back the note and started the car. I was biting my lip. "Six months. He didn't give you long."

"No."

"So... that's why you've got Gaby pumping Sandy."

He nodded.

"Well, I don't know about Anne's other man, but I can tell you this. She was found with only seven dollars in her purse."

"It doesn't mean anything. The killer would have taken it, assuming be was the one who'd given it to her."

I turned the car around and drove back toward Curt's place. He didn't have to say he wanted my help. He'd been saying it all morning, in a dozen ways. The next move was mine.

"Let's say Frankie didn't do it. Why do you think the killers still around'?"

"Several reasons. Bernice is one. Her situation was a lot like Anne's."

"Oh? In what way?"

"She had a roving eye, Gil says. A truckdriver friend of his was making it with her for a year. After he left town, Gil went out to see if she wanted a replacement."

"Gil Sisk?" I felt a hot flush of jealousy. "Gil wouldn't want Bernice."

"A feminine viewpoint. Gil said she had a number of interesting... features. No brains, but Gil wasn't wanting conversation. Anyway, she gave him the cold eye, so he decided somebody had beat him there. Could've been Anne's old boyfriend."

"Curt, that's too farfetched."

"Not if you add up the other similarities. Forget Anne was your sister, look at her objectively. She was roughly the age of Bernice. Had the same kind of passive, unexciting husband. She was known to advertise what she had—like Bernice. And at the end she and Bernice both had a secret lover—"

"Oh Lord!" I gasped. "I just remembered, Bernice was in the store a couple of days before she was . . before she died. She'd been saving trading stamps, but this time she waved them away. She said there were better ways of getting gifts, and besides she'd be leaving town soon. That's like Anne telling Frankie she could get a big wad of money. What do you think?"

"It fits," said Curt. We were approaching his place; Gil had gone, probably to lunch. Neither Gaby nor Lou had come back.

"Park behind the house," said Curt. "I want you to talk to Heine a minute."

Heine had shut down his drilling rig and was getting ready to leave for lunch. Heine was a living insult to Hitler's Aryan ideal; short and stooped, with large hairy arms hanging to his knees. He had a dark, wizened face and wiry, tight-curled hair. He also had a local monopoly on well digging, sewer cleaning and plumbing.

"Heine, tell her what you found when you went out to the Strubles' place the day after she drowned."

"What I don't find, you mean?" Heine gave me a black-toothed grin. "My big pipe wrench. Gone. I think somebody steal it. Maybe the sheriff." He winked at me.

"Did you look in the well?" asked Curt.

Heine's eyes widened. "Ah, that well, we fill her up."

"Why?" asked Curt.

"Mister Struble, he said fill up quick, to the top. This is custom, to fill up the wells when people inside fall. Always. Water is no good to drink."

As he drove away, I said to Curt: "You're taking a lot for granted, even if the pipe wrench was in the well. Okay, it could have been a weapon. But you don't know she was murdered, you don't even know she had a lover—"

"No." He sat down on the steps of the wooden porch. "Her husband took a room in town and left her stuff in the house. I'd like to go through it, see if there are any notes, flowers, souvenirs from her lover." He looked up at me. "Struble listed his place with your husband. That means Lou has a key, right?"

I felt my back stiffen. I knew what was coming. "Yes."

"Can you get it for me?"

"Why not ask Lou?"

"A month from now I could. Right now I don't know him well enough."

I looked out, trying to frame my answer. I saw a car approaching, kicking up a long serpent of dust. Gradually I made out the sheriff's emblem on the side.

"Get in the house," said Curt.

"But why—?"

"Go on. I don't want you to cramp the sheriff's style."

I went in and looked out the window; I felt resentful, not because I'd been sent inside, though that was part of it, but because Curt had obviously planned this when he had me park behind the house. I was being used as... what? An impartial witness? An ace in the hole? How did he plan things so far in advance?

The car parked at the foot of the hill, near the crumbled foundation of a barn. Sheriff Wade got out, followed by Deputy Hoff. I felt a thrill of fear for Curt as the two men strode up the hill. Deputy Hoff was the sheriff's nephew, but they looked enough alike to he father and son: hulking thick-necked men, with the deputy slightly taller and broader than his uncle. He'd left off wearing his theatrical forty-fives and now wore a .38 in a holster clipped to his belt, just like the sheriff.

Curt greeted them without rising from the steps. "Howdy, Shurf," he said in an exaggerated drawl. "What brings you out to these parts?"

The sheriff's white teeth showed in a humorless smile. "Drop the humor, Friedland. You ain't Chester and I ain't Matt Dillon. We came out to look around."

"Look away," said Curt, waving at the barren hills. "I see you brought Deputy Hoff, whose fearless gun is all that stands in the way of Franklin County being drenched in the blood of innocents."

Deputy Hoff hunched his shoulders. "Now listen, Friedland—"

"Easy, Bobby," said the sheriff. To Curt he said: "You was just a kid when you left. They say you're smarter than your brothers, but so far you ain't showed any signs of it. You got a rumor started I railroaded your brother to the pen and I don't like that a little bit. You got the county saying the Struble woman got shoved in the well, and her old man's tearing his hair. He ran to me, and I had to go through all the evidence with him again. Now I'd like to know what business you've got in this county."

"That's none of your business, sheriff."

The deputy blurted: "Uncle Glen, let me—"

"No Bobby, he's right. Legally it's none of my business. One thing that is, Friedland, and that's if you got any firearms in that house."

Curt rose slowly. "I didn't know the state had a Sullivan law."

"I don't know what they call it. All I know is I gotta register all the firearms in the county."

"Well, just out of curiosity, how many have you registered so far?"

The sheriff's face froze in surprise, just long enough to convince me there was no such law. His features quickly smoothed over. "That's none of your business, boy. You gonna let us see them guns?"

"I'd like to see something first. Something like a search warrant."

The sheriff's neck reddened. "You aim for me to drive to Franklin for a piece of paper while you stash the guns out in the brush?"

"You can leave Paladin here to watch me." Curt walked slowly down the steps. I couldn't see his face, but his voice look on a strange, velvety menace. "You're not afraid to stay, are you Bobby? I'll set up a target so you can practice with your shootin' iron. You need it, Bobby. Anybody who hits a man in the back when he's aiming at his legs—"

"You better shut your goddam trap, Friedland."

"You did aim for his legs, didn't you Bobby? That's what you said at the trial."

"One more word, Friedland—"

"Go to the car, Bobby," said the sheriff.

"Let him stay." Curt stepped onto the graveled area in front of the steps. "He can leave his gun on. It doesn't scare me. Any son-of-a-bitch who can't shoot better—"

Bobby tore his gun front his belt and snarled. "I don't need a gun for you."

He rushed Curt, starting his wide swing while still a yard away. Curt sidestepped and seized the arm. I saw a blur of movement, then felt the earth tremble as Bobby thumped onto the ground. He lay gray-faced, trying to get his breath. He sounded like a truck trying to start on a cold morning.

Curt backed away as Bobby rose. "The Japanese call it The Gentle Way, Bobby. Judo. The harder you come the harder you land."

Bobby charged with a roar of rage. This time I heard the air whoosh out of his lungs when he landed. Twin streams of dark blood trickled from his nostrils. As he got to his knees, I saw that the sharp gravel had ripped his shirt. Dark patches showed where the blood had begun to soak through. Bobby stood up and shook his head like an angry bull. Blood smeared his face on either side of his nose, giving him a garish crimson moustache. He took a step toward his gun, but the sheriff snatched it up.

"*That's enough!* Bobby, get the hell back to the car."

Bobby stumbled off, wiping his nose on his sleeve. The sheriff drew the gun from its holster. "Curt, I'm gonna have to arrest you."

Curt seemed relaxed, his voice mildly curious. "What's the charge, Sheriff?"

"Disturbing the peace."

"Whose peace? Look around. I'm on my own property."

"You assaulted an officer of the law."

"Hell! He assaulted me."

"I doubt the judge will take your word against mine and Bobby's." He jerked his head down the hill. "Better get moving."

Curt didn't turn his head. "Velda," he said in a conversational tone.

I drew a deep breath and stepped out onto the porch.

The sheriff was taken by surprise, and in that instant I saw... more than I wanted. I saw the eyes of a man who'd killed more than once, and I saw the same look his victims must have seen. A glazed, animal violence. Something inside me shriveled up and went into hiding.

"Your husband know you're here, Velda?"

"No... but I suppose he will."

His face turned cunning. "Not from me, Velda. I know better than to tell a man what his wife does behind his back." He peered at me as though he'd never seen me before. "I thought your sis was a black sheep, the way she rubbed up against trouble. Now I'm thinking maybe it runs in the family."

He slid Bobby's gun back into the holster and looked at Curt. "I arrested you a minute ago. Now I'm releasing you for lack of evidence. You're free to leave the county any time."

"I'll go when I'm ready."

For a moment the sheriff's face held a look of sincere regret. "Yeah, I figured that. You want to be pushed."

I watched the sheriff walk down the hill and drive off. I felt weak and sick at my stomach. I must have staggered because I felt Curt's arm slide around me. I wanted to lean, and lean hard, but I pulled away. "I've got to go."

We walked around the house to the car, and I said: "You deliberately provoked that fight, Curt. They could have come bearing roses, and you'd still have fought. Why? Just tell me why?"

"I had to see them with the wraps off. I wanted to read them in a hurry."

"Did you?"

He nodded. "Bobby's matured some. Twelve years ago he'd have charged me a lot quicker. But still a boob. He's like a dog the sheriff keeps on a leash, valuable because the honky-tonk cowboys are scared of him. The sheriff is smart, but he's been in office too long. He's trapped in details and can't see the forest for the trees. Honest enough—that is, if you offered him a bribe he'd gun-whip you half to death. On the other hand, if he got the word from a respected citizen—just a calm and thoughtful discussion of a particular case—it could turn him off a suspect without leaving him aware that he'd been influenced." He opened the car door for me. "They're typical rural cops, a little on the rough side, a little gun-happy. They're helping the killer, but they don't know it."

I slid behind the wheel. "Otherwise they'd have killed you the first chance you gave them. Did you think of that?"

He gave me a half smile. "Yes. I thought of it."

I met his eyes and I saw that he didn't care. I saw what he meant when he said he'd taken the jump into darkness. He was no longer responsible for his own life. I got a chilly, crawly feeling. I could only think that in not caring about his own, he couldn't possibly care about the lives of others. Especially mine.

I looked out through the windshield. "Curt, I... can't give you Struble's key."

"I... understand."

"No... no you don't. I can't help you, I can't get involved. Maybe I sympathize with you. I think you're doing something great. But I've got a husband, a daughter. I can't get mixed up in it. Please don't get me mixed up in it."

He nodded gravely. "If that's the way you want it."

"I do." I turned the switch and started the car. Curt leaned against the window.

"Just one question, Velda. When Marston got killed on the tractor, why did he go into the ravine twenty feet from the end of the row? Was he drunk? Did he fall asleep? Why didn't he jump clear?"

I stared at him with my mouth open. I could feel the blood drain from my face. "How did you know?"

"I've got reports on every death in the county for the last twenty years. Indexed and cross-indexed. If you'd like to see—"

"No, no! Curt, you promised—"

"Okay. But think about it, will you? Did Marston have any enemies? Could somebody have knocked him out and set the thing up? And Ethel's husband , why didn't he jump out of his stalled car when the train was coming? He could see two hundred yards in both directions. He had no record of heart trouble, he didn't drink. Think of Don Carroll, who accidentally shot himself on his front porch? And Harold Simpson, who supposedly committed suicide in his house. Why would he leave his tractor out in the middle of the field, the way you do when you have a visitor you know won't be long? Think about those things, Velda. Picture a guy who's killed... eight-ten people in the last twenty years. A guy who knows that if you watch and wait long enough, you'll be able to make it look like an accident. Think of him watching you, waiting for his chance...."

I drove off, squirming inside. The day had turned overcast, with an icy wind. It fitted my mood.

The empty house did nothing to ease my mind. I took a warm bath, but it failed to induce my usual somnolent, lazy mood. I darkened the studio and played the piano, and my thoughts drifted to Marston....

Mart was a big, open-faced, good-humored lout who'd been my brother's best friend. He'd teased and pinched and tickled me all through my youth, and the teasing had evolved gradually into caresses, then love. That last spring he'd worked on the farm where we planned to live after we were married. I always packed his lunch and ate with him on the grassy bank beside a stream. That last afternoon, we'd finished lunch and were smoking a lazy cigaret. Mart was saying he had to get back to work, and I was saying of course, and both of us knew we'd make love first because we did every day....

Later, lying on the blanket beneath the branches of a box-elder tree, I held his weight and pressed my fingers into his back; I felt his warm breath against my neck, and noted how the leaves overhead were green and glossy on top, pale and fuzzy beneath. My mind was sunk deep within my body, following the slow surge of sweet sensation—

Something flickered at the edge of my vision. "Mart!" I said.

He raised his head. His pupils were pinpointed.

"Mart, something flashed in that grove of trees on the hill."

Abruptly I was alone, bereft and exposed. I sat up and pulled my dress down over my legs, Mart was standing, hooking his overalls with angry haste. I watched him leap across the stream and scramble up the bank. He loped toward the trees and disappeared behind them. Five minutes later he returned, red-faced and sweating.

"Some kid," he panted. "I just got a glimpse."

He wouldn't meet my eyes, and I knew he'd lied about something. "You didn't see who it was?"

"No," he said too quickly. "You better go now."

I left, feeling a sour emptiness inside me. How could those evil spying eyes spoil the happiness I'd felt? But they had; I felt dirty, sinful and sneaky. I visualized how I'd looked to those eyes: Sprawled and impaled by a hulking, hunching animal with greasy overalls pushed down to his knees. I had a feeling I'd never enjoy sex with Mart again....

And I never had, because he'd been found dead that afternoon. The shock had erased all memory of the prying eyes until Curt had brought up Mart's death. Now I wondered: Could the flash have been binoculars? Not many kids had binoculars. And if a man, wouldn't he fear that he'd been recognized, and couldn't he have knocked Mart out somehow, laid him in the ditch, and turned the tractor over on him?

Sixteen years, I thought. What clues survive after sixteen years? Long ago there might have been a chance; now it was pointless, hopeless speculation....

Sharon came home at five, breathless and excited. She'd met Gabrielle in town and they'd had a coke together and talked. Now Sharon had sworn off dates and resolved to spend her nights studying shorthand and typing. She planned to go to Chicago and become a career woman just like Gaby....

Lou called from Connersville at five-thirty and said there was a new road going in and he thought he'd stay and bid on the dirtwork since he had a couple of idle bulldozers. Sharon and I ate alone, then watched television and went to bed. I took a Seconal tablet, which I rarely do....

zzzzt... zzzzt... zzzzt ... ZZZZT ... ZZZZT!

The ringing dragged me struggling from an ocean of sleep. I shot upright with thoughts of disaster exploding in my mind. The illuminated alarm clock said twelve-fifteen. Lou was asleep, stretched out like a corpse with his nose aimed at the ceiling.

The phone broke off its staccato message. I jumped out of bed and raced for the kitchen with my nightgown streaming out behind me. I lifted the receiver and heard the operator's shrill voice:

"...pronounced them dead on the spot. The three oldest will live but—"

"Who, Sally?" I shouted over a babble of voices. "Who died?"

"George Bennett's house burned down an hour ago. Sandy died in the fire along with her baby—"

My stomach lurched. I dropped the receiver into its cradle and pressed my hands to my head. *He doesn't care*, I thought, *He doesn't care who he kills, women or babies....*

My husband's snore echoed softly through the silent house. I walked into Sharon's room. She was asleep, her full lips pouting, the covers kicked down around her feet. Her pajama top was twisted, and a round, womanized breast peeped through. Sharon made me feel vulnerable and exposed. I pulled the blanket over her and walked to the window. The darkness hovered outside like a threat. I pictured a pair of loathsome, inhuman eyes looking on, watching—and I knew I couldn't sit on the sidelines.

I pulled the drapes and went back to the phone. To the operator I said: "Give me the residence of Curt Friedland."

CHARTER THREE

Curt's phone hadn't been connected. I hung up the receiver with a feeling of loneliness I couldn't quite understand. What could Curt have given me? Reassurance that it wasn't murder? Confirmation of my own horrible dread that it was?

I wasn't sure, but still I wanted to talk to him. I pushed open the back door and stepped out. The chill air penetrated my thin nightgown and tingled on the flesh beneath. I went back in the bedroom and got my housecoat; Lou still lay corpselike, his snoring unbroken. I slipped on my houseshoes and walked back outside. Lou's red pickup gleamed in half-moonlight just a couple of yards from the back door. I brushed my hand over the cool metal of the hood and smelled the faint odor of gas. I started toward the garage where my car was parked—

"Velda, what's the matter?"

I turned and saw Lou in the door in his pajamas. There was my husband; I should go to his arms and be comforted, instead of chasing off in the middle of the night to see a man I hardly knew.

I walked back and told him: "There was a line ring. Sandy Matthews... Bennett was burned up in their house. Her little baby too."

Lou sucked in his breath. "Poor George. How'd it happen?"

"I don't know."

He was gone from the door. I heard him in the kitchen ringing the operator, then talking. Muffled fragments of conversation came to me: "...totally destroyed? Yes... sure, something will have to be done for them. Get me Harley Grove. Harley? Listen, you know about the Bennetts? Yes. The kids can stay with Mrs. Thompson, I'll make sure it's okay. No, George didn't have any insurance... I held the mortgage... Sure, insured to the extent of the mortgage but it's a total loss to George... get a collection rolling... I'm good for five hundred, well, hell, but it's all we can do...."

I tuned out his voice. This is the way it's done, I thought. Smooth over death with normal activity, samaritan gestures; forget the charred bodies and the monster who lurks in the night....

Lou was behind me again. "Well, I've done what I can." I resented the smugness in his voice. *Lou, death is not a husking bee....*

"Better come to bed, Velda."

"I will... in a minute."

His arms went around my waist, his hands slid between the lapels of my housecoat and pressed against my bare stomach. His breath blew warm on my neck. "I'm pretty sure of getting this road job, Velda. Then I'll be working hard..."

I understood then. My husband's sexual enthusiasm waxed and waned according to no rhythm I could figure; not the moon, not the seasons, not the rise and fall of his business fortunes. Lately he'd gone through a virile phase; now he was serving notice that we approached a period of celibacy. To him Sandy's death was a community event; it had nothing to do with us.

"Lou, I couldn't tonight... really."

His hands squeezed, then trailed away. Only a painful after-tingle told me that he'd squeezed hard; that he was angry with me. "Good night, Velda," he said.

I couldn't go to Curt now. Lou would sleep lightly for at least an hour. I went into the bedroom and lay down without speaking to Lou. I remember smoking my fourth cigaret, then it was daylight and Lou's bed was empty....

I drove to town earlier than usual and asked Ethel to take over the store again. I had to bear her rheumatic complaints and her lament for poor Sandy, who was somehow related to Ethel. She agreed finally, but I could see I'd have trouble with her later.

At first I thought Curt's place was deserted; Heine Wentz wasn't there, and Curt's car was gone. Then I saw Gil's black Chrysler convertible parked behind the house. Gaby and Gil stood on top of the hill, at the archery range. Gaby looked gay and windblown in a halter and white short shorts; she *did* have a figure, that girl, and the shorts did nothing but accent the sharp thrust of her buttocks. Gil wore a red shirt and tan slacks; he was obviously not dressed for working today. I felt a tingle of annoyance as I approached them; they stood too close together, and I thought that Gaby should be told about Gil's reputation. Somehow learning that Gil had tried to seduce Bernice had altered my opinion of him. I watched Gil's arrow hit the target several rings out from the bull's-eye, and I wondered if he was using Curt's bow. (I already felt possessive about Curt's things, even his wife.) They were laughing when I went up, but when Gaby saw me, her face turned sober.

"Where's Curt?" I asked her.

Her face became wary. "I think he went to town."

"I just came from there," I said. "He isn't there."

She was looking at me with the question in her eyes: *What do you want with him?* She had a right to it, I guess. Any girl coming back to her husband's home town would wonder: What was this woman to my husband in the past? How well did they know each other? Who do I have to watch and who can I ignore?

If we had been alone, I would have explained it all to her; now I only said:

"He asked me to do something for him yesterday. I told him no. I want to tell him I've changed my mind."

"Oh." Her wary expression didn't lift; her eyes slid over to Gil's and then back to mine. "You... could check where the house burned clown. He might have gone there."

I should have thought of that first. The Bennetts lived on the river bottom just a half mile from town. George worked at the lumberyard; his land was water-logged gumbo which rarely produced anything but fifteen-foot-high horseweeds. A dozen cars were parked along the lane which led to the house; a crowd of sightseers trampled around the ruins. It had been an old wooden house, with imitation brick siding made of tar paper; it must have burned like a torch. A pall of smoke still hung over the area. I saw two blackened, twisted iron bedsteads, a refrigerator shining blue-gray where the enamel had flaked off, a cookstove and heating stove. Only these items stood erect; all else was a foot-deep layer of smoking rubble inside the foundation walls. I searched the crowd for a familiar face. By the sheriff's car, in the center of the largest group of people, stood George Bennett. He wore no shirt, and his sleeveless undershirt was full of charred holes. Soot blackened his heavy face. I moved closer. Beside him stood a boy of about eight, George's oldest boy, looking wide-eyed at the sheriff while his father talked in a flat grating monotone:

"—You can put it down to that, Sheriff, if you got to have a reason. That goddam kerosene stove. I could kill myself for not fixing it."

"What was wrong with the stove?" asked the sheriff.

"Got a tank on the back, you know. There was a little drip right where the tubing connected to the tank. Time went on, it soaked the floor behind the stove. Last night was a little chilly, so I had the stove lit. I reckon that's where it started."

"Why couldn't your wife get out?"

Heads turned to see who had asked the question, but I didn't have to look. I recognized Curt's voice. He didn't look as though he'd gotten any sleep last night either. His trousers and sweatshirt were wrinkled, and a faint blond stubble glistened in the sunlight. The sheriff saw Curt too, but for some reason chose not to call him by name.

"You folks out there shut up and let me ask the questions." To George he said, "Why couldn't Sandy get out?"

George looked down at his feet. "Well... she come in last night around ten-thirty. She'd been drinkin... quite a bit. I knew she'd left the house without a cent that morning so I tried to find out who bought her liquor. She went to sleep without tellin me. I jumped in the truck and went in to Stubb's to find out who'd got her drunk. The tavern was closed. When I came back to the house the fire was shootin up higher'n them cotton-woods. My three oldest kids was in the yard. I couldn't get closer'n thirty feet of the house. I... stood, and... watched the goddam roof fall in on... Sandy and the kid... Jesus Christ, that goddam stove... "

Sober faces watched George Bennett push through the crowd with his forearm over his eyes, then a voice said; "I know who got her drunk."

I saw Johnny Drew, Anne's ex-husband. I was surprised, because he'd left town a week ago saying he was going to work in Las Vegas. He was dressed in a checkered sport jacket and powder-blue slacks, and he looked garishly over-dressed in that austere rural gathering. There had been a time long ago when I'd thought he was handsome, as handsome as Johnny himself thought he was. But that had been before I noticed the finger waves he pressed in his waxy blond hair, before I saw the smallness of his eyes and how close set they were in a coarse peasant face. Since Anne's death he'd drifted in and out of Sherman; he'd served a ten month sentence on a bad check charge and once he'd tried to hold up the Club 75 with a pistol. Lou had smoothed that one over, perhaps because Johnny was an ex-brother-in-law. He certainty hadn't done it for me, because I had only contempt for Johnny. I noticed his red eyes and the lank strand of blond hair hanging over his eye and I knew he was half-drunk already. Everybody else was looking at Johnny, including the sheriff, but nobody asked any questions. They knew Johnny didn't have to be coaxed to tell everything he knew.

"He's the one," said Johnny, pointing a blunt finger at Curt. "I saw 'em together last night in Stubb's tavern."

Curt frowned at Johnny, perhaps trying to place him. I heard mutters in the crowd. *Who's that? Who got her drunk? Curt Friedland. When did he get back?* Behind it was a low murmur, like far distant thunder, with nothing in it of friendship or neighborliness. Johnny Drew must have felt the hostility too, because he took a step toward Curt with his fists doubled at his sides.

"I thought the country was rid of the Friedlands. Maybe you need another lesson."

A faint flicker of a smile crossed Curt's face. He neither moved forward nor backed away. I don't think he expected Johnny to come for him, and I don't think Johnny intended to—but suddenly the crowd parted and left a channel leading from Johnny to Curt. There was nothing for Johnny to do but lower his head and charge. But he stopped suddenly, confronting the massive gabardine-clad torso of the sheriff. The sheriff knew Johnny too; he didn't even raise his hands in front of him. Suddenly there was Deputy Hoff behind Johnny, who cramped Johnny's arm behind his back and marched him to the car. It didn't look to me like Johnny was struggling; it all seemed to go off half-heartedly, like a stage production in which the actors aren't enthusiastic about their parts.

The sheriff turned to Curt. "Now. Is it true what he said?"

"Partly."

The sheriff sighed. He spoke for the crowd, not for Curt, in a tone of sweet reasonableness. "Why can't you just say it? Did you get Sandy drunk or didn't you?"

"I bought her a beer in the tavern. I left her at seven-ten. She wasn't drunk then."

"How do you know it was seven-ten when you left her?"

"I looked at a clock."

The sheriff looked at him sadly a moment then turned to the crowd. "All right folks, let's clear out of here. We all got work to do. Doc Chalmers says Sandy and the baby probably suffocated from smoke before the flames got to 'em—"

"What about the man who got her drunk?" It was only a voice; I couldn't see the face.

"I aim to look into that, but I'm afraid that's between him and her husband. It's no crime to buy an adult woman liquor."

He started toward his car, and I was close enough to hear him tell Curt as he passed: "You seem to hang around trouble, boy. Be careful they don't haul you out in a box."

Then he got in his car and drove away, with Johnny Drew glaring at Curt from the safety of the back seat. I started toward Curt, but he was striding rapidly toward his car and people were watching him go and I... I was reluctant to put myself next to him. I was afraid of my reputation in the community, and ashamed of myself because I was concerned about that now. I hurried along a few paces behind him, and he was in his car and gone before I reached him. I told myself, Velda, you'd better stay out of this affair if you're afraid of getting dirty....

I half-expected him to come in the store later, assuming that either Gaby or Gil had told him I wanted to see him. Bat he didn't. I thought of going up to his place, but I'd already done that. By nine o'clock that evening I couldn't wait any longer; I called and Gaby answered the phone. I almost hung up; I didn't like to look like I was pursuing him. But I'd started it already, so I asked:

"Did... Curt come back?"

"He stopped in around four."

Silence then. She was making me work for it. "I wonder... did you tell him—?"

"Yes." Her voice still held the wariness I'd noticed earlier. "I said you'd changed your mind. He said he'd get in touch."

That was it; that was all she could tell me. I wanted something else; my relationship with Gaby was extremely uncomfortable; I was like a business acquaintance and yet I had no business calling Curt. I was about to say something friendly, something which would get our mutual conversations off the exclusive subject of Curt when I heard a man's muffled voice and Gaby's equally muffled answer, as though she'd put her hand over the mouthpiece.

"Who's with you?"

"Gil Sisk," she said.

"Oh... well, goodby." I hung up the phone, feeling resentful. Here I was ready to help Curt and...

Lou came home around ten and wanted to talk about the new job. He seemed in a bright, gay mood and I wondered why, until I figured out in my head that he'd made a couple thousand off the sale to Curt and probably stood to clear ten thousand on the road job.

Next morning the town prepared for the funeral; all the stores would close at noon, and services would be held at one p.m. I heard some resentful talk about Curt from those who knew he'd bought her that beer. They had nothing to go on, but I could feel their latent hostility. If a tornado wiped out the town they'd find a way to blame Curt Friedland because it happened while he was here. That's the kind of reasoning you run into in Sherman....

About ten Curt strolled in with his face closed up tight, his hands shoved deep into the pockets of his Levis. He wore a wide-brimmed felt hat, blue-denim jacket and lace-up boots: he looked as though he'd never left the Nation. I started to speak but he shook his head emphatically and asked for a can of Velvet. He handed me a bill with a note in it. I opened the cash register, spread the note out in the dollar-bill tray and read: MEET ME AT THE BOY SCOUT CABIN ON LAKE PILLYBAY AT ONE P.M. DESTROY THIS.

I started to say that was the time of Sandy's funeral and it would look bad if I didn't go, but he walked out without even taking his change. Gladys Schmit stood at the door and I knew by her expression she wanted him to say hello so she could offer some schoolteacherish advice. Curt went out without seeing her. Gladys's eyes turned cold and I knew he'd lost another friend....

I locked up at twelve-thirty and drove straight out to Lake Pillybay. Curt's caution had made me wary; I knew how it would look if my car were found parked along a country road—new cream-colored Lincoln with sparkling chrome and white sidewalk. Lou had picked it out. I pulled off the road and hid the car behind a clump of hazel brush. I climbed to the top of a ridge and approached the cabin from the rear. It lay at the head of a little cove which was rarely used by the tourists, having a steep shore-line and no gentle slopes on which to build summer cabins. The cabin itself was crudely built of logs, used on summer weekends by our Boy

Scout troop and the rest of the time by assorted tramps and lovers. The relics of the latter were very much in evidence when I got there; bottles and cans and cigaret butts, so I moved to the side of the water and sat on a rock. It had turned warm, and I took off my sweater and sat in the sun. As I waited, I thought: I should have brought a book, or some knitting. The very idea made me laugh aloud. I was excited and trembling inside. I didn't realize how nervous I was until Curt's voice spoke my name and I jumped at least six inches in the air. I turned and saw him approaching from behind, carrying a flat manila envelope in his hand. By the time he reached me I was calm enough to say:

"I was wishing I'd brought my knitting."

He sat on the ground beside me. "I checked to see if you might have been followed. Took me some time to find your car. Good job."

I felt a faint thrill of gratification. "I could take up bird-watching, carry binoculars and a bird book. That would give me some excuse to prowl the hills alone."

He studied me narrowly, then: "You're kidding, but it's something to keep in mind." He picked up a pebble and tossed it into the water. "Gaby said you'd changed your mind."

I looked down and stirred the dead grass with my foot. "It's not that cut and dried. I want to know more. Particularly about Sandy, whether you think she was one of his victims."

"I'm almost sure. I checked with Stubb Dixon at the tavern. He said she left at eight o'clock, about forty minutes after I left. She wasn't drunk then, so she must have met a man with a bottle."

I nodded. "Sandy had a habit of riding with whoever made an offer. Marriage didn't change that."

"Yes, it could have happened this way: the guy took her home, waited until George left the house, then went in and set the house afire. Or it may not have been the killer who took her home, just a guy who happened to see her. The killer could have been watching the house, waiting for his chance. I looked around, but the crowd had wiped out any sign of tracks. Her body was so badly burned there was no way of knowing how she'd died." He shook his head. "That couldn't be luck. The guy is smart as hell...."

"Why were you with Sandy?" I asked.

"Gaby drew a blank. Sandy kept hinting that she knew something...."

"She's been hinting for twelve years."

"Yes, anyway I met her, and she was still playing coy, wanted me to meet her the following afternoon. We made a date, but she was killed that night."

"I think she was playing you along," I said.

Curt shrugged. "Maybe. But she had certain things in common with Bernice and your sister. Married, playing around on the side. The guy might choose married women because they've got as much reason to hide an affair as the man. Unless they fall in love, that is, then they're likely to say the hell with everything and bring it all into the open. That would give him a motive for murder."

There was excitement in being near a man who burned with a purpose aside from making money and having fun. I wondered if I was really interested in finding the killer or if I just wanted to stay close to Curt and absorb some of his fire; I also knew that I had to give him something in return.

"You seem so certain of murder, Curt. I'd like to know why."

"Got it right here." He tapped the manila envelope. "But let's get out of the open."

I followed him away from the lake shore. Bending down, we entered a crab-apple thicket; the lake was hidden by tall dry grass. We were screened overhead by the brushy twigs of the crab apple. I laid down my sweater and sat on it, drawing my legs up beneath me. Curt sat down beside me and for a moment I wished there were no murders, that we were just lovers who'd come out into the woods with a picnic lunch and a blanket. Curt gave me a curiously penetrating look—as though he'd caught my thought—then bent his head and opened the envelope:

"It's kind of dry and statistical. Are you sure—?"

"Yes. But one thing I'm curious about first. Where were you last night when I called?"

He looked off into the distance. "Searching Gil Sisk's house."

I gasped. "Gil's *house?*"

He nodded. "The night Sandy was murdered... well, let me go further back. There's a hill about a quarter mile away from our house. It's the only one nearby which has a view from a higher level than our house, a natural lookout if somebody wanted to spy on me. So I took some black thread and fastened it to trees and bushes so it ran around the top of a hill at waist level. Sheep and dogs and wild animals could go right under it. A cow or deer couldn't, but they'd leave tracks. Well, the morning after Sandy's murder, the thread was broken. I found footprints, not sharp to identify, but obviously a man's. There were signs that he'd stretched full length and rested his elbows on the ground as though holding binoculars—"

"Why?"

"The marks were side by side. If he'd been holding a rifle, one elbow would have been behind the other, like this." He rolled onto his stomach and demonstrated. I felt a chill, remembering the flash on the hill while Marty and I... If only someone had investigated, before the passage of so many years....

"How did that involve Gil?" I asked.

"Well... I'd noticed that Gil carried binoculars in his car. He said they were for girl-watching on Lake Pillybay, which sounded reasonable—"

"Considering Gil's character," I said dryly.

"Yes, but I wanted to check. So I searched his house; I was looking for some... relic which would show he'd had something to do with these girls. That's a weird old house, you know—thirty-eight rooms, and I barely got started. There's something in every room, going all the way back to his great-grandfather. It was like taking an inventory of the Smithsonian in a single afternoon. I didn't find anything, but I'd like to finish; I'd like to clear him of suspicion—"

"Why?"

"I like him."

"I don't."

He smiled at me. "Since you heard about Bernice?"

"Maybe."

"He also had a few brief sessions with Anne and Sandy. He made no secret of it with me."

My face burned. "The more I learn about him, the more I realize our friendship was a mistake."

"You're jealous."

"I don't think so. Disappointed..."

He laughed. "Velda, you give a man friendship and you expect it to fulfill all his desires."

"It's enough for me."

"It's a different situation. Think what would happen if the reproduction of the race depended on women. How often do they take the initiative?" He shook his head. "Anyway, you don't understand a man's approach. All the time Gil was talking to you about books and philosophy and everything else, he was looking at you and wondering how you'd be in bed, trying to figure out a way to get you there...."

I looked at him and wondered if he was doing the same, but I didn't say it. I said: "You don't believe that. Otherwise you wouldn't have left Gaby there alone with him."

"Gaby's trained. She knows all the approaches. Anyway she had her own game going; she had to keep him occupied until I got back from searching his house. She couldn't submit, because that would have used up her ace in the hole."

I stared at him in amazement. "You're *really* throwing in all you've got, aren't you?"

"What do you mean?"

"I mean... if Gil is the killer, you're risking Gaby's life."

"She has a gun. She knows how to use it."

"She wasn't wearing it yesterday with him, not concealed under her halter and shorts."

He frowned. "I'll tell her to be more careful. But even if Gil was the one who watched the house, he could be a simple garden-variety Peeping Tom. He's taken with Gaby; obviously, since she's a woman. We didn't have curtains up then, and Gaby was sprinting across in front of the windows in the altogether...."

I felt a prickly embarrassment hearing Curt talk of his wife. For a moment I saw them in the intimacy of their home, doing what husbands and wives do, what Lou and I do on occasion. But was it embarrassment, or jealousy, the kind I'd felt about Gil? What did I want, for every man in the county to worship me from afar and be true? A high school attitude, Velda....

I said, apropos of nothing: "Lou was home when Sandy was killed."

He looked at me sharply. "What made you say that?"

"Just... in case you suspect him."

"I suspect everybody—except myself. When did he get home?"

"He was in bed asleep when the call came about Sandy."

"There would have been at least a half hour delay between setting the fire and the line ring. How long had he been home?"

"The engine of his pickup was cold."

His eyebrows shot up. "You *checked* it?"

"I just happened to put my hand on it." My face burned. "Curt, you don't think I'd spy on my husband!"

"No, I didn't think so." He sighed. "Well, somebody killed her right under my nose and didn't leave a clue. We'll have to go back to the others." He pulled the papers out of the envelope. "Here, if you're still interested."

I glanced at the pages dense with figures and printing. "Curt, I'm not a statistician. Just tell me."

He took the pages from my hands. "Okay. Consider four hundred people living in Sherman, another eleven hundred in the surrounding farms. That's fifteen hundred people. Now here... He pulled out a printed sheet. "I've got actuarial tables on accidental death. Scaling it down to Sherman's size, you'd expect something like thirty accidental deaths during the last ten years. We've had forty-two."

"Maybe we're accident prone. It isn't an ordinary community."

"Okay, consider that. Go back ten more years, we're only seven percent above the national average. Go back ten more, we're exactly average. And so on, until we get back to where they didn't keep statistics. We're an average community in everything else. We have fewer deaths from smallpox, influenza, typhoid fever, and so on, just like the nation as a whole. We have more deaths from automobile accidents, slightly more than the nation as a whole. Suicides have gone up nationally; so have they here... but a little more than average. General farm accidents, household accidents, sporting accidents, we're ten to fifteen percent above average."

"What does it mean?"

"Some of them are murders disguised as accidents."

I stared at him. "Curt, I don't have your faith in numbers, I guess. I can't—"

He handed me a sheaf of papers. "Read these and then tell me. They take you back twenty years."

I read:

Lester Lemonn, 53, died of broken neck after car struck loose gravel on shoulder of highway. Presumed he swerved to avoid livestock. (Comment: Steering gear could have been tampered with. No record of autopsy, or of car having been examined.)

I looked up. "Curt, you're not counting this sort of thing, are you? I mean, there are so many accidents."

He nodded. "That's right. So damn many. I'm assuming we have an average number of accidents. That leaves a dozen which were really murders. Go on, read."

I went on:

Sally Niven, 32, found hanged in henhouse. Children at school, husband working. Presumed suicide. Apparently climbed up on box and kicked it away. Motive for suicide: depression, money problems. (Comment: Left no note, no record of having threatened suicide. Situation easily staged, possible rape-murder.)

Theodore Groner, 15, drowned. Swam for boat in middle of cove, apparently suffered stomach cramp. Witnesses in boat; Jerry Blake, Eli Black, Marston Odon, Gil Sisk, Rally Cartright, Louis Bayrd, Johnny Drew, and Harley Grove. (Number of witnesses make accident probable, but stomach cramps unlikely, since water was warm and victim had eaten nothing but peanuts for some time before swimming. Subsequent death of two witnesses Marston and Jerry, suspicious.)

Charles Hall, 19 and *Ruth Payson*, 16, killed when car struck semi-trailer head-on. (Many possibilities here: jimmied steering mechanism, driver drugged with delayed action soporific.)

I looked up. "You mean a sleeping tablet which doesn't take effect until later?"

Curt nodded. "Most of them don't hit you for ten minutes anyway. Put an extra-thick gelatin capsule around it, and it might take a half hour longer. They ate hamburgers at the Club 75 before starting home. The driver could have been drugged then. Hall was known as a fast driver."

"How do you know all this? It happened seventeen years ago."

"Files of the county paper. It's a small enough community so that every death rates a three-column spread."

I returned to my reading:

Marston Field, 22, killed when tractor turned on him. Crushed chest cause of death. (But, he could have been knocked unconscious beforehand, as there were several bruises on him. Ravine was several feet from end of row. No witnesses.)

Anne Groenfelder Drew, 25, found with throat cut outside Club 75. (Murderer still at large.)

I passed those two without comment. We'd been through them already.

Arnold Shaw, 24, and *LaVella England*, 21, asphyxiated in parked automobile. Found in half-dressed condition, presumed that leaky muffler had let fumes seep through floorboard. (Comment: Could have been murdered by attaching hose to tailpipe, running it through bottom of car. No indication that muffler was checked to see that it actually leaked. Couple could have been unconscious when scene was staged, via pills. Double suicide ruled out; couple was engaged and had no problems.)

"But Curt, *two* of them?"

"The killer was probably after only one, but he doesn't seem to care if others go too. Look at Sandy and her baby; the baby just happened to be there."

The next was:

Marvin DeVore, 38, killed in cement mixer. Assumed that he'd gotten shovel caught in it, reached in to get it without shutting down machine. Presumably his clothes caught and he was pulled up inside. Immense weight of rolling cement on blades crushed and mutilated his body, inflicted several deadly wounds. (Comment: Official of cement mixer company states that he's never heard of a man being *drawn* inside from ground level. Falling in from a higher level, or being thrown in, conscious or unconscious, would probably have been fatal. Condition of body precludes accurate determination of cause of death.)

Barney Proctor, 45, killed by train in rural crossing. Engineer stated the car was stopped at crossing; fireman thought driver was slumped over wheel, but wasn't sure. Theory: He'd stalled his car at the crossing, seen the train, and suffered a heart attack. Autopsy revealed nothing; body too badly shattered. (Comment: A farfetched chain of circumstances. Equally reasonable to assume the man was knocked unconscious and his car driven on the tracks. Convenient means of concealing evidence.)

Jerry Blake, 40, died when butane tank exploded in his store. Verdict: accidental death. (Comment: Takes time for butane to accumulate in sufficient quantity to explode. Why didn't Blake smell it? Store burned down, body burned beyond recognition. Cause of death therefore uncertain.)

I looked up. "Curt, I knew Jerry very well. He was Lou's partner. He was the kindest, best-natured guy in town. It's unthinkable that he was murdered—"

"Consider the unthinkable, Velda. Jerry could have learned something, and the killer had to silence him. Don't worry about motive, look at similarities, the mutilation of the bodies. Read on."

I read:

Harold Simpson, 38, died of shotgun blast in mouth. Verdict: suicide. Wife had left him, taken children. Depressed. (Comments: Left no note. Tractor left standing in field, as though he planned to return to work. Blowing a man's head off with a 12-gauge shotgun is effective way of concealing murder by other means.)

Dean Slaughter, 55, suffocated when storm blew barn down, haymow collapsed and buried him in baled hay. Verdict: accident. (Comment: Check it out. Too neat.)

I jerked my head up. "Curt, how in the world could you suspect *that?"*

Curt shrugged. "Hell. The killer could have seen the storm coming and smothered him before the barn ever blew down."

"And then blew it down himself?"

"He could have hammered some rafters loose and weakened the barn enough that a good wind would blow it over. Sure, it's far out. If there's nothing to connect his death with any of the others, I'll mark it off and work on the easier ones."

I glanced down at the next one:

Albert Simmons, gored to death by bull in barnyard. (Probable accident.)

"Probable! Now Curt, really—!"

"It could have been arranged. The man knocked unconscious, the bull goaded. Simmons owned the bull, you think he'd take any risk if he knew the bull was dangerous? If you've ever seen a bullfight, you'd know how easy it is to goad a bull into charging. The killer probably had plenty of time; here in this sparsely populated county, half the people die unseen. How many deaths are listed as heart attacks which were really murder? I didn't even include heart attacks, but I know there are drugs which overstimulate the heart. Say our killer knows his victim has a weak heart; he introduces a drug into his food and pouf! Without an autopsy, who knows? That sheriff is so damn considerate of other people's feelings he won't cut up somebody's next-of-kin without permission. Go on to the next one."

Maynard Schoentgen, 62, body found partly devoured by hogs. Presumed cause of death, heart attack.

"You see?" said Curt. "This man could have died from strangulation, stabbing, or anything. This is like the train wreck, like the fire and the cement mixer, all the evidence has been obliterated."

I felt a strange coldness at the back of my neck as I went back to my reading. The sheer weight of evidence was beginning to convince me:

Adlai Neilsen, 42, died in plane crash five minutes after takeoff from pasture landing strip. County officials, CAB, ruled death accidental through malfunction of aircraft. (What caused malfunction of aircraft? Unknown.)

Ben Burger, 54, and *Elbert Sim,* 60, found dead from exposure. Both known drunks, left tavern with bottle during blizzard, presumably passed out in cold. (Comment: Could have been followed, drugged.)

Vera Ballinger, 43, electrocuted by massage machine. Short found in wiring. (Comment: Be wary of electrical mishaps unless they're witnessed. Death can occur any place, then the business arranged to look like an accident. This includes following:)

Bryon Danley, 40, electrocuted in home welding shop. Working alone, late at night, found next morning.

Bernice Struble, 21, dead in well, death by drowning, while unconscious. Unconsciousness induced by striking head on bricks; hair and pieces of scalp found there. (Comment: Difficult to see how glancing blow could produce unconsciousness. Also more likely she'd lose her footing while pulling up the bucket, rather than after she'd pulled it up. Another shaky chain of circumstances.)

That was all—except for poor Sandy, who hadn't yet been added. I handed the papers back to Curt and felt a cold shiver pass up my spine:

"Curt, that kind of thinking scares me. If there are people like this, then nobody's safe. I'll be suspicious of people who come into the store; afraid to let Sharon stay out late. It's like... a wolf following a caribou herd, waiting to pull down the cripples. Like a snarling beast lurking outside the circle of light."

He was putting his papers away. "He's there, Velda. He looks just like anybody else, just like you and I."

"Look, I know we're backward in Sherman, but at least we're *civilized.*"

"Sure. The French thought they were civilized with their gold tasseled cushions and learned debates in the Sorbonne. At the same time Giles de Rais was killing 2,000 people, almost depopulating a province of France. Only 60 years ago in Chicago a certain Doctor H. H. Holmes confessed to killing twenty-seven people in a single year. Actually they figured he killed over a hundred—and he sold their skeletons to medical schools."

"But this man ... you say he's been twenty years..."

"He's smart. So far there've been only doubts. Doubts pass. People forget."

"But what could be his motive?"

"I think we make a mistake in looking for a motive. It could be anything. He wanted to kill, he built his own motive. Maybe he wasn't even aware of what he was doing; he worked himself into a position where he had to kill simply because he wanted to kill."

Suddenly I glanced at my watch. I was used to having the afternoons creep by; I was amazed to see that it was four-thirty. Sharon would be coming home in a quarter hour; now of all times I wanted to be near her and assure myself she was safe. Even the woods seemed prickly and hostile. I picked up my sweater and wrapped it around me. "Curt, I've got to go."

"Yes." He rose and put his manila envelope under his arm. His face wore a watchful, waiting look. I knew what he was waiting for.

"I'll help you if I can Curt. But don't ask me to take any risk. Not that I'm scared; I mean, certainly I'm scared, but I've got more than myself to think about."

He nodded. "There's something you can do. Take some of these cases. Anne was your sister. Jerry Blake was your husband's business partner. Marston was your fiancé. Ethel works for you. Find out all you can without seeming too interested. I don't want him to get suspicious."

"But... what am I supposed to be looking for?"

"I don't know. Some common denominator. Something that ties them together. Somebody they were all intimate with, or somebody they'd all had trouble with. I don't know... It seems ridiculous that he got away unseen every time. If we find out that the same person happened to be nearby when two or three of the accidents occurred, we'll have something to go on."

Just before we parted at the top of the ridge I asked Curt: "You still want the key to Bernice's house?"

"It's better than breaking in."

All right," I said. "I'll try to have it tomorrow morning."

I drove home and picked up Sharon, telling her I had to come back to the store and work on the books. In the store I talked to Ethel, trying to find a casual way of bringing up her husband, but there was no need. Ethel had gone to Sandy's funeral; her mind had been turned to thoughts of death:

"So few people there, Velda, I couldn't help but think about Barney's funeral. Churchyard full of people standing, I was just sorry it was a closed casket, poor Barney was so cut up. I remember cars parked all the way down to the river bridge from the cemetery. He had so many friends."

"What was he doing the day he died?"

"Fishing. You know he'd rather fish than eat, that man. There was a water hole under the railroad bridge, where he usually went with Gil Sisk, who never had much to do, or Johnny Drew, who could have done a lot but never did. Barney didn't care much who went with him as long as there was fishing involved."

"Were either of them with him that day?"

"No. Johnny got mixed up in a dice game down behind the depot and Gil... funny, I remember that day just like it was yesterday. Gil stopped by the store to say he couldn't make it because he was going to Kansas City, but Barney had already gone. Gil didn't even know Barney had been killed until he got back a week later.

At home I thought about it. Both Gil and Johnny Drew had known that Barney planned to fish under the old railroad bridge. Gil had also gone unexpectedly to Kansas City the night Anne was killed. And Gil had sometimes helped Mart on the farm; they were the same age, and had run together all through high school. Gil had known that I brought Mart's lunch to him. (What about those binoculars, that girl-watching on the lake? Tie that in with the glint of glasses on the hill.)

The thought upset me. Even though I was disappointed in Gil, the thought of him being a murderer... that would imply that I'd been totally blind—

Johnny Drew was another matter. As prospective brothers-in-law of similar age, he and Mart would be expected to be friends. But it hadn't worked out that way. Johnny Drew used it as an excuse to borrow money from Mart. He also knew about the farm and the fact that I brought Mart's lunch. The day Mart was killed, Johnny had been drinking in a tavern. Nobody had kept track of his comings and goings. He'd been connected with Jerry Blake too. He and Lou had hired him to work in their store, but they'd had to let him go. Lou hadn't told me why, but I'd assumed he'd either been stealing from stock or from the cash register. Lou and I never discussed my brother-in-law if it could be avoided; it left a bad taste in my mouth. But Johnny was one person who could have approached Anne's car outside the Club 75 without alarming her. That was the same night Johnny—Oh God! What horrible tricks the subconscious plays. He'd tried to rape me that night, and I'd completely forgotten about it. Now I recalled him banging on the door at ten p.m. Sharon had been asleep and Lou had gone to Omaha with a cattle shipment. "Where's Anne?" he yelled. "Where is that goddam woman?" I could tell through the door that he was drunk. I told him to go away or I'd call the police. He calmed down and asked if I could just let him in, because he wanted to call the club and see if Anne was there. I was young and naïve then and I let him in. The moment I opened the door I knew I'd made a mistake. His eyes were glazed and red-rimmed; it was clear that he was too drunk to see. He made a grab which tore my nightgown off my shoulder; he called me a dirty name which I'd heard him use on Anne. I told him I wasn't Anne, but he was past hearing. He was ripping the nightgown right off my body and I made the mistake of trying to fight him. All I had were fists and fingernails, and Johnny was so drunk that only a bludgeon would have stopped him. Finally I gave up trying to fight; I tore myself free of the nightgown and left him holding it. I ran into the bedroom and slammed the door. He pounded on the door awhile and cursed me—he was still calling me Anne—then he wandered outdoors. I locked all the doors and windows and called Lou's hotel in Omaha; Lou had gone out to eat and so I told the operator to have him call back. I went to sleep beside the phone and Lou called up at three a.m. He said the clerk had forgotten to give him the message when he came in and what was wrong? I looked out the window and saw that Johnny's car was gone and the danger was over; I felt like a foolish, hysterical girl and said I just wanted to talk. So we'd talked—briefly— and next morning Anne had been found dead and I'd forgotten all about Johnny's visit. But I remembered that Johnny liked to sit in taverns and tell anybody who'd listen what a great Jap-killer he'd been in the islands. . .

Excited, I got Curt on the phone. His first words dampened my enthusiasm:

"Velda, listen, just remember that this is a party line. Okay?"

"Oh." Suddenly I sensed a dozen ears listening. I'd been using the party line for years and it had never bothered me before. "Well, remember what you said about looking for a common denominator? I've found one: Johnny Drew."

"Got it. Thanks." He hung up, and so did I. I felt disappointed; phone calls were so unsatisfactory.

Lou came home at eight, tired. He'd gotten the road job and had been out all day with surveyors. I drew his bath and fed him supper and waited until he was snoring softly. Then I snagged his key ring off the bureau, and carried it into the kitchen. I found one key with a tag taped to it marked *Struble*. From my own key ring I took a similar key, switched the tags, and put it on Lou's key ring. Then I tiptoed into the bedroom and replaced Lou's key ring on the bureau. If somebody else wanted to see the Struble place tomorrow... tough.

I got in bed and felt a hundred little nerves quivering in my body. I thought of taking a Seconal, but no, that would make me groggy tomorrow and I needed all my alertness.

Lou still lay with his nose pointed at the ceiling, the blanket pushed down past his hips. Black hair stood up in tufts between the buttons of his silk pyjamas. There was a wall in my mind blocking me off from what I'd just done; I didn't want to think about it.

I was starting my second cigaret when Lou's voice said: "Velda."

There was no inflection, nothing. I was sure he'd seen me. I thought, How will I explain it, what excuse can I possibly give him?

"Yes?"

"Why don't you come over here?"

I felt relief. So... that was it. He'd gone to sleep, rested a bit and perhaps had a dream... there was no explaining his urges, perhaps there was no explaining those of any male.

"It's... late," I said.

"You weren't asleep anyway, were you?" No need to answer that; he'd known I wasn't. "Don't come if you don't want to."

Thank you, Lou. But then I knew I'd feel guilty; here was a man who worked hard to provide a nice house and luxury and all the money I could spend....

I slid out from beneath the covers and stood on the mat between our beds. I seized the hem of the nightdress and pulled it off over my head. The air felt cool on my body.

I sat down on the edge of the bed. He didn't move. There is a mental-physical shorthand, a combination of movements and attitudes which comprise the unspoken sexual language of long-married people. I knew what he wanted. I put my palm on his stomach, felt the thick matted hair press against my pain.

"Put the light out, please," I said.

The light went out. In the dark, I can sometimes pretend I am on the black gelding, riding through the night with the wind in my face. This time it didn't work. I felt guilty because I was glad when it was over.

Next morning at ten Curt came into the store and asked for a can of Velvet. I rang it up and gave him his change. With it was the key to the Struble place. He raked it smoothly off the counter and slid it into his pocket.

I said: "Are you—?"

He stopped me with a quick shake of the head. He pointed to his ears and then at the walls, the stacks of canned goods. I understood then; he was afraid of hidden microphones. I took out a piece of paper and I wrote: *Are you going out now?*

He shook his head, wrote under it: *For Gaby, to stand watch.*

I will, I wrote.

Again he shook his head and put down one word: *Risk.*

I wrote: *Pick me up back door one-half hour.* Then to choke off further argument, I crumpled the paper and shoved it in my apron pocket. He lifted his shoulders, then nodded and walked out.

He was waiting in the alley a half hour later. I locked the back door—Ethel had her own key to the front—and stepped into his car. I hunched down between the front seat and the dash, regretting that I hadn't thought to wear slacks. I had to hike my skirt up to my hips to stay hidden, but it didn't matter; Curt looked silently ahead as be drove out of town. His old car sent exhaust fumes up my nose; I was perspiring, probably from excitement. I felt like a juvenile sneaking out on her first date. After a long time Curt tapped me on the shoulder and I sat up, gulped fresh air, and took the cigaret he handed me. We were on a rarely-used dirt road which crossed the river via a rattle-trap steel bridge and met the gravel road which passed the Struble place.

While he drove, I asked him about Gil Sisk and Johnny Drew.

"I haven't cleared Gil yet," he said. "And Johnny Drew seems too stupid. If he were in a city he'd be a small-time hood running errands and trying to look like a big-shot torpedo. Here he's nothing. Anyway, he's dropped out of sight. Maybe the sheriff scared him out of the county. I've spent the last two nights scouring his old hangouts, but nobody's seen him."

He slowed as we passed the Struble house. In the back yard I glimpsed the mound of naked earth which covered Bernice's next-to-last resting place. He turned off the highway and onto a dirt track leading toward the river. Our tires crackled on the sticky gumbo. Patches of ice lay beneath the trees—all that remained of snowbanks. He stopped beneath the cottonwoods and switched off the engine. A curve in the lane hid us from the road. "Now," he said, "we follow the river until we come to a hedgerow. Then we follow that up to the Struble house."

I stared at him. "How do you know so much about it?"

"Aerial photos," he said. "I bought copies from the outfit which surveyed the county last year. Next time you come out to the house I want you to take a look at them."

I stepped out of the car and saw immediately that my heels wouldn't make it. I took off my shoes, then peeled off my hose too. Curt stood waiting, and I flushed with guilt because I was slowing him down. Gaby would probably have had the foresight to wear flats and jeans. As we walked on, the icy mud crawled between my bare toes and reminded me of the high school walkouts we used to take on the first warm day of spring.

Silently we made our way up the hedgerow to the house. Curt left me crouched beneath a spirea bush while he opened the front door with his key. I was to whistle like a bobwhite —the only bird I could imitate—if I saw anybody coming. I couldn't seem to get comfortable; spirea bushes spread out impossibly close to the ground, and a slick mound of ice remained beneath them. I squatted with my bare feet sliding on the ice—feet which had once been calloused but now were soft and tender—and I felt the cold ascend like water percolating upward, reaching my ankles, my calves....

It had reached my thighs when Curt reappeared and said, "Let's go." I followed him on legs which were stiff as stilts, down to the hedgerow, where I again slowed him down because I had to beware of thorns. When we reached the river he started on, then he looked back at me. I was red-faced, sweating, and puffing, so he found a clump of willows and said: "Here, let's rest a minute."

We sat down and lit cigarets, and I asked: "Did you find anything?"

"Nothing, which is significant in itself."

"Why?"

"All her things were there, receipts, appointment slips, matchbook covers, hairpins, perfume, photographs and letters and everything else relatives take when they go through the effects of a deceased person."

"So?"

"So her relatives hadn't gone through it. But someone had. Her things were jumbled, disarranged; the lining of her purse was ripped loose. The sheriff didn't search, I'm sure; he didn't even suspect murder."

"It must have been the killer."

He nodded. "Another scrap to add to the evidence that she was killed. I was nearly certain of that already." He looked at me. "Ready to go?"

"I... guess."

Maybe because there was disappointment in my face, I don't know, but he bent down and touched his lips to mine, very lightly. At least I suppose it was a light touch, even though I felt an electric current passing through my body. I must have been in a sensual state from the mud squishing through my toes, or the excitement of our stealth, but I had to remind myself that I shouldn't, mustn't slide my arms around his back and press him against me. I kept telling myself *no no no* until he drew back his head. I looked at him and I regretted that his eyes... that he had trained them so well that they showed nothing of what he felt. When he spoke I didn't have the faintest idea what he was talking about....

"It's a way station, you know. A point in a journey to a destination. If we're not going to make the whole trip, we shouldn't even get on the train."

I realized then he meant the kiss. I was aware of the leaves arching overhead and the river flowing by at our feet, brown and muddy now with the flow-off from melted snow, and I thought, Well, who's getting off? Then I realized he'd said this in order to give me time to think, so that I'd know exactly what lay ahead. So I thought of Sharon and Lou... and Gaby too, and all the people who would be involved, and I said, "Then I guess you'd better not kiss me again."

He stood up and held down his hand for me. In his eyes I saw that I'd dissembled too late. I read the knowledge that I was available, willing, that he had only to provide a time and a place and the proper conditions. I knew that later, in an hour or a day I would be grateful to him, but now I was only disappointed and angry at myself for being so vulnerable....

I rejected his hand and got up by myself. We walked toward the car in silence.

Ten feet from the car he stopped and motioned me back with a violent gesture of his hand. I watched him tiptoe forward, peering at the ground. He took a piece of paper off the windshield where it had been held beneath the wiper like a traffic ticket. Then, stepping in his same tracks, he came back to me and unfolded the paper. It was a penciled note which said: GET OUT OF TOWN OR GET KILD. TAKE YOUR CHOISE.

"Stay here a minute," he said.

I stood holding the note while he searched around the car in ever-widening circles. He walked out to the road and then back. "Gone," he said. He squatted clown and looked beneath the car, then got a long stick and released the catch on the hood. Without touching the car he examined the engine. Then he poked the stick through the open window and pressed the starter. The car grumbled and lurched, then stopped. I let out my breath, slowly, and only then realized that I'd half-expected an explosion.

"Okay," he said. "Get in. But don't step there."

He was pointing to a sharply defined track in the soft mud. I looked at it and then looked at Curt. "He left a footprint?"

"A beautiful footprint. Too beautiful."

I frowned. "Why?"

"It's probably a red herring. Look here." He placed his foot beside the print. The other mark extended an inch beyond his shoe. "I wear tens. This must be a twelve. And the ribbed sole is like they put on engineer's boots. It's all too distinctive, too traceable to be real."

"What are you going to do?"

"Take you back to town, then go home and get my plaster and make a cast of the print. It's something to look for, even though the shoes are probably buried someplace by this time."

We were driving along the gravel when I said: "Well at least the note narrows it down. You know the man's illiterate."

He threw back his head and laughed. "Sure, it narrows it down. It tells me the man is a damn sight from being illiterate. Look at the note. He can't conceal the fact that he's used to printing. So be uses his left hand to write the note. Make an 'E' with your fingernail there." I did. "See? You made the vertical bar and the bottom horizontal bar in one motion, then attached the other two horizontal bars. That's the way this guy did. A semi-illiterate who draws his letters would make the vertical bar and then the three horizontal bars all separately. Now notice how his right-handed habits carry over. Make an 'A' with your nail." I did. "Okay, on the left diagonal line, you started from top to bottom, then retraced the line back to the top and came down again to make the right diagonal. So did this guy. You can see the double line. The slant shows he wrote it left-handed, but as a matter of fact he was right-handed, otherwise he'd have done the right diagonal first. Same with the 'V' and there's the 'E' again. See what he's told us about himself?"

I looked at Curt. "What?"

"Not a damn thing... except—" He paused and frowned. "Except that he understands the game. This note accomplishes no purpose at all except to make the game more interesting for him. Now he's expecting me to carry this note around the county, searching for matching paper, trying to get samples of handwriting. . ." He laughed abruptly, took the note and shoved it in his shirt pocket. "Yes, he understands the game."

I stared at Curt. "Is that all it is to you? Just a game?"

He turned to me, and there was a strange glitter in his eyes. "Life is a game, Velda. It ends in death. So does this. Now we could get bitter and morbid about it, or we can relax and swing—"

"Or we can check out."

"*You* can. You want to?"

"No." I said it quickly, without thinking, but I realized I meant it. "It just seems to me you've got the odds against you now. He knows you, and you don't know him."

"I will someday."

"When? How?"

"When he tries to kill me."

"Suppose he succeeds."

"That's my game," he said. "To see that he doesn't."

CHAPTER FOUR

I expected Curt next morning but he didn't show up. I was disappointed because I wanted to know if he'd learned anything from the footprints. Gaby came in around eleven; before we knew it we were talking on a level of honesty which I'm sure neither of us intended. That was during our conversation at the cash register; there was a cold drizzle outside and Gaby wore a hooded black raincoat which made her took drawn and tired. I remarked that she was no doubt working hard getting moved in—the kind of social babble you carry on while you're ringing up purchases—and Gaby said she was. I asked if Curt was getting the place fixed like he wanted and only then did I realize that I'd forcibly turned the conversation to her husband.

"He... hasn't been home much lately," said Gaby.

I looked at her and saw a flicker of terror in her eyes, a look which told me she was younger than I thought and had never encountered this kind of problem before. She covered up quickly by throwing back her hood and fluffing out her hair with a quick shake of her head. Then she said:

"At least it's better than having him get bored. When he gets bored he kicks everything to pieces just to see it fly apart."

I didn't want to go that deeply; I pulled back. I asked with a smile: "What does he break up, furniture?"

"No. That was his brother Frankie's specialty, breaking up bars and things. Curt's more subtle." She looked down and fiddled with her billfold, snapping and unsnapping the catch. "He got bored with his research firm, and that's no longer operating. He got bored living with a certain couple while he was going to college and when he left they got divorced. Toward the end they weren't speaking to each other, only to Curt. You'd never get him to admit he had anything to do with that, but I think he did. He's that way about human relationships. He sees a social setup the way a mechanic might see a motor, and he sort of..." she made a fluttery motion with her hands, "...jiggles the wires around to see what will happen."

Suddenly I realized she didn't understand Curt, even though she'd been trying for oh, how many years? She'd built up a vast store of knowledge about his reactions to given situations, but he was still a stranger to her, like an unknown animal in a cage. You know that if you stand around cracking your knuckles, it will turn ferocious. Though you don't know why it turns ferocious, therefore you can't say you understand it, at least you can deal with it. He likes long hair, he hates polished toenails, that's the sort of thing she knew about him.

I had her groceries boxed now and her change made, but she wasn't through. She lit a cigaret and gave me a level look.

"He's had affairs before, you know."

The words sent an electric shock through my body. I felt the heat rise to my face, and at that moment I was sure she knew about our visit to the Struble house and our kiss by the river. *Before* was the key word, that's what made her words apply directly to me—and at the same time made me feel like an insignificant figure at the end of a long line of women. The girl was clever, in spite of her youth.

"Has he?" I asked. "What did you do?"

"Waited. They didn't really compete with me. No more than a... supermarket competes with a gas station. He goes to them for something different than he gets from me."

"What?"

"Excitement, the game, the chance to work out his mind on somebody new—"

"And sex, naturally."

She shrugged. "It isn't the important thing. He never chases a woman for sex. If he does, it's not because he desires them."

I was interested, now that we'd left the specific and gone on to the general. Also I was puzzled. "What reason could he have?"

"To... uh, experiment. To see how sex will affect the woman, or his attitude toward her." She shook her head. "I don't know, really. I just know he's been with women he could have had and he hasn't touched them. Others... vice versa—until he learns what he wants."

"And then what does he do?"

"The same as he does with other people he has no more use for." She held up her palm and blew across it. "He banishes them."

"Banishes them?"

"Doesn't see them. They talk, their words don't reach his mind. He treats them politely, remotely and totally impersonal. I guess there's nothing more frustrating. You can't fight it. Women get drunk and swear at him. He acts surprised. I think he really is because he doesn't realize what he's done to them. When he can't use a person any more, they cease to exist."

I knew what she was doing; she was giving me fair warning: *He wants you only to use you, and here's what'll happen when he gets through with you.* Yet I felt no hostility from her. We were like two housewives talking over a mutual problem; Gaby having the more experience with the problem, she'd led the discussion: *Be sure to whip your egg whites and fold them in separately....*

Sharon came in then and bloomed like a flower when she saw Gaby. I received a perfunctory Hi Mother, then the two went next door to the drugstore. I envied Gaby at that moment—not for her intimacy with my daughter, for a mother gets used to being regarded as dowdy and middle-aged—but for her ability to switch personalities. It wasn't faked; one moment Gaby was an adult woman talking to me about adult matters, the next moment she was a teenager skipping off to discuss records and boys and dating. Gaby was a chameleon, changing her attitudes and personality to suit her environment. I saw that Curt need never tire of her; all he had to do was put her in a new environment and he'd have a new woman....

Gil clomped in for Missus Friedland's groceries. I caught a sour smell of beer on his breath and knew he'd come from the tavern. (I'd begun noticing unpleasant things about him which I'd missed before.) Sarcastically I asked if he and Gabrielle weren't on a first-name basis by now.

"Well now Velda, that's only when we're alone. A smart man never lets on he's high winner in a crap game."

That annoyed me too; not to mention his fake country accent. Immediately I connected it with the note which had been left on Curt's windshield. As Gil walked out, I stared at his shoes. They were big, at least number twelve. I wished Curt would come in so that I could talk to him about Gil. I still couldn't imagine him leaving Gaby alone with a man he really suspected.

The belt tinkled, but it was only Ethel. She took off her raincoat, put away her purse, cleaned her spectacles, and each move was accompanied by a soulful sigh. I didn't ask her anything, I just waited. Finally, after another gut-wrenching sigh, she said: "I didn't sleep hardly a wink last night."

I was supposed to ask why, so I did.

"Thinking about poor Barney. He was always so careful at crossings. And his eyesight was so good—"

"Then how do you explain the accident?"

"He must have been, you know, despondent. He liked Mart a lot, and he never got over finding him dead underneath the tractor."

I felt a chill climb my body; I'd forgotten about Barney finding Mart's body. I must have gone pale, because Ethel asked me what was wrong.

"I was wondering," I said. "Did Barney mention to you that he'd found anything there, or seen anything?"

Ethel looked puzzled. "I'd have to think... "

"Well, think then."

"Why do you want me to think about that?"

"You mentioned that Bernice might have been murdered. Did you ever think your husband might have been?"

Ethel's eyes went wide and round behind the glasses. "Velda! What a terrible thing to say! I won't hear another word." And she wouldn't. She got busy cleaning out the meat cooler and didn't raise her head until I left. I didn't particularly want to go home, but Curt knew my schedule and that's where he'd expect to find me.

I found nothing to do in the house. I would have gone riding but I didn't dare in case Curt called or came by. I was going through all the hardships of a clandestine affair and having none of the fun.

Four o'clock came, and a phone call. Curt's voice said: "Jamboree tomorrow at one p.m."

"What—?"

But he hung up even before I finished the first word. I replaced the receiver with annoyance. Jamboree. What kind of crypticism was that? I puzzled for five minutes, then remembered that Boy Scout conventions were called jamborees. Of course, Curt wanted me to meet him in the Boy Scout cabin....

At noon next day Ethel came in tight-lipped and hollow-eyed.

"I'm quitting, Mrs. Bayrd."

"Ethel, what's the matter?"

Sincerity was evident from the tears in her eyes. "There's no need to talk me out of it, I won't stay in this town another minute. I'm going over to Franklin and live with my sister. She's alone in the house and she's been wanting me to come for a long time."

"Well, of course, if that's what you want. But why?"

"There's something bad going on in this town. Don't ask me, because I won't tell you."

But it was not Ethel's nature to be silent. In the process of getting her things together—I did persuade her to work just one more afternoon— she said that around midnight she'd gotten a phone call. No words were spoken; just a man's voice imitating a train whistle, then laughing. Next morning she'd found a toy train on her doorstep. It had come from a child's playpen next door, and had frightened Ethel to death. "...Just think of the man out there, putting that train on my doorstep... lurking around all night watching and waiting. I couldn't stay another night...."

I mentioned that this proved there was something strange about her husband's death. Why didn't she go to the sheriff? She gave me a hard, narrow look and said: "Maybe it does, maybe it doesn't. Barney's dead and that's it. Being alone you learn you can depend on nobody but yourself. My mind tells me to forget it and that's what I'll do. Whatever you're doing, don't bring me into it. If you do—" her voice became plaintive, lost and weepy. "I'm not a young woman, Velda. I just want him to let me live in peace, that's all. . ."

I left before she started crying on my shoulder. I went out to the lake, parked the car in the same hiding place but approached the cabin from above.

A hundred yards away I sat down behind a clump of buckbrush and waited for Curt to appear below. I'd been there ten minutes when a pair of hands seized my shoulders and jerked me backwards. I arched my back and started to kick when I saw Curt's face grinning down at me.

"Just thought I'd give you a little lesson in camouflage. Don't try to hide in vegetation while you're wearing a blue dress."

Speaking of dresses made me aware that mine had balled up around my thighs. I sat up and pulled it down over my legs. Curt brushed off my back and I could smell pipe tobacco on his breath.

"I thought the killer had me," I said.

"Then you should have screamed," he said. "Best weapon a woman's got is her voice. If you're grabbed, let out the loudest, most blood-curdling screech you can. That usually startles a man enough to make him lose his hold, then you can run."

"Where I grew up a scream didn't do any good. We lived a mile from any neighbors. What's that?"

He'd sat down beside me and pulled out a newspaper clipping. "Front page of the latest county paper. This item here interests me."

A good part of the front page was devoted to Sandy's death, but almost half a column concerned a burglary of the sheriff's office, written in the tongue-in-cheek manner which journalists always use when the police are victims of crime.

IS HIS FACE RED?

A burglary of the courthouse last Sunday night left an embarrassed sheriff seeking an acrobatic burglar who entered the sheriff's office through a third-story window. The sheriff believed it was a prank by a group of boys. Items stolen were:

1. Kit of burglar tools taken from traveler from Minneapolis.

2. Bogus check signed U. Ben Hadde, made out to proprietor of Eat-Rite Cafe.

3. Twenty-two caliber bullet taken from sheriff's arm, received during arrest of auto thief thirteen years ago.

4. Photographic file accrued during the sheriff's 28-year term of office.

5. Fragment of safe blown open at Farmer's Credit Company.

6. Six shares of stock in Reliable Oil Company, a nonexistent firm, which were purchased by various county residents.

7. Assorted pornography impounded from prisoners.

8. Wanted poster for John Dillinger which had hung in office since 1933.

9. Assorted knives, blackjacks, knuckle-dusters and instruments of mayhem lifted from combatants during various peace disturbances.

I looked at Curt. "What does it mean?"

"Item four is the important one, you can forget the rest. I wanted those photos. The one of your sister's body would have been there, so would Mart's and Bernice's and... hell, everybody else I'm interested in. I was trying to figure out a way to get them but the killer beat me to it. Taking that other stuff was a blind, to make it look like a prank." He sighed and folded the clipping. "Well, at least I've got him busy covering up his tracks. One of these days I'll catch him at it." He looked at me. "Anything new?"

"My free afternoons are shot to hell for awhile," I said. "Ethel quit this morning."

When I told him why, Curt looked thoughtful. "I think I see his game. It fits what Gil told me."

"What?"

"He got a call last night, man said it wasn't healthy to work for Curt Friedland, then hung up. Gil called the central switchboard but they had no record of the call."

I frowned. "How could that be?"

"With our old-fashioned party line you can hook onto the line somewhere out in the country and call a person without going through the switchboard. You know how you call others on your line without going through central."

"Yes, but... do you believe Gil?"

He looked at me. "Why not?"

"Well... there's his reputation with women, and the fact that he knew where Mart was working, where Barney was fishing, and so on.... Besides, he wears about size twelve shoes."

Curt lit his pipe in a preoccupied manner. "I made those casts, by the way. The indentation could have been made by a 220-pound man—or by a 160-pound man carrying a 60-pound load."

I shook my head in amazement. "You never accept the obvious, do you?"

"Can't afford to. Gil, for example... the guy is such an airy figure here in the community, nobody notices his comings and goings. Gil's vague about where he goes when he's away... which proves not a goddam thing, because he's vague when he's right here." He stood up. "I'll walk you back to your car. How strong are you?"

"Strong enough to walk," I said, getting up.

"That's not what I meant. Those phone calls could mean he's trying to isolate me, turn the community against me. He might work on you next."

I set my jaw firmly. "I'll let you know when I turn against you. When do we meet again?"

"I don't know. Your afternoons are out, the night..."

I felt a bitter frustration. "What do I do, just exist in limbo until you call?"

"The problem is—look, can you give me a key to the store?"

"Well... I guess. What for?"

"I want to search for bugs. Microphones. That's the only way he could have known you were working on Ethel, by listening in. Once I clear that up we can talk there."

I opened my purse and got out my key ring. Then I stopped. "When are you going to search?"

He shrugged. "Midnight. It's a good hour."

"I'll come and stand watch."

"I won't need it. I'll work in the dark."

My face went hot. "Look, I know I was the one who didn't want risk. But I'd rather be doing something than sitting at home."

After a moment he nodded. "Okay. Wear dark clothing. Go in the back door. Don't turn on any lights. I'll knock once and you let me in. You keep the key, it's safer."

We reached my car and I started to seize the door handle. Suddenly he grabbed my arm and jerked me back. "Wait! Now you get another lesson. You see anything strange about your car?"

My neck hairs rose as I looked it over. Shiny chrome, polished glass, gleaming enamel, all covered by a thin patina of road dust. Someone had written across the door: VELDA BAYRD IS A HORE.

I felt rage pinch my nostrils. "Son-of-a-bitching kids—!"

"Not kids," he said. "Look at the lettering."

I looked, and my rage turned to a chill. The writing slanted backward just like that of the note.

"I see. He knew where we were."

Curt nodded. "He's starting on you, Velda. Better not come to the store tonight."

I set my teeth. "I'll be there," I said. I was scared, but I was mad, mad enough to go after the killer with my bare hands and fingernails....

Curt wouldn't let me in the car until he'd gone through his routine of checking for booby traps. Then he searched for car tracks but the gravel road revealed none. As I drove off—he was going to stay and search the woods—I could feel hidden eyes watching me. I knew why Ethel wanted to run; it was a terrible feeling.

The night began badly. I'd made the date assuming that Lou would be asleep by midnight, but midnight came and Lou hadn't even come home. I didn't want to leave Sharon alone, so I waited. Lou came in around twelve-thirty and said he just wanted to go to bed. I mixed him a drink and he fell asleep before he finished it. I pulled on navy-blue slacks and stuffed my nightdress inside them. It made me bunchy around the hips but I wasn't going to a fashion show. Over that I put a black cardigan. I'd backed into the garage beforehand—I was getting skilled at stealth—so I had only to release the brake and coast down the drive to the gate before starting the engine.

I pulled into the alley behind the store with my lights off. The dashboard clock said one-thirty. It was an eerie hour: the town was dark and silent and a chilly wind whistled around the corners of the buildings. I stopped outside the back door. If anyone saw me I planned to say that I'd come back to lock up the office safe. Curt stepped from a doorway, almost invisible in black. He whispered:

"Go in and close the door. No lights."

I went in and closed the door behind me. The only light came from a streetlamp on the corner. I listened to the sound of my breathing and the hum of the meat cooler. The store was warm and full of familiar smells, but in the dark it seemed alien. I jumped as a knock sounded at the back door. I opened it; Curt was silhouetted in the door a moment, then he stepped to one side and disappeared. I closed the door and turned, trying to penetrate the blackness.

"How can you see?" I whispered.

"Another lesson in skulking, Velda," he said. "Use your peripheral vision. The corner of the eye. Look over there at the cash register. You see me clearly?"

"I see a lumpy shadow, yes."

"Okay, now look toward my voice. I disappear, don't I?"

He did. The next thing I knew he was standing so close I could feel the warmth of his body. My muscles went taut and quivery, expecting his touch. But he didn't move. We stood in darkness amid the odor of celery and cold meats. Curt seemed to be listening. Finally I asked:

"Shall I stand at the front and watch the street?"

"No, you watch the back. Gaby's parked where she can see the front."

"Oh." I felt strangely disappointed. "She knows I'm here."

"Yes," said Curt, moving away. "I'll start with the cash register. The electric system would be a good place to hide a microphone."

I stood by the back door for what seemed like a half hour, listening to the occasional tinkle of metal. I could tell when Curt left the cash register and started tinkering with the meat cooler. The silence prickled at my nerves; when Curt came near enough so I could communicate in a whisper, I asked why he'd quit having Gaby watch Gil Sisk.

"Too risky," said Curt. "Anyway, if he's the guilty party, I want to give him a chance to incriminate himself. He has no really ironclad alibi for the time of any of these accidents, and that's what makes me—"

He was interrupted by two short honks of an automobile horn. "That's Gaby's signal," said Curt.

We hurried out the front door and into the street. A half block away stood Curt's car and Gaby beside it, looking down at the ground. The car looked squat and low to the ground, and then I saw that the rear tires were flat.

"He did it while I was watching the store," said Gaby. "The wind was rattling the leaves in the park, and I didn't hear a thing. But he must have been crawling around the car while I sat there—"

"Your car," Curt told me. "We'll go out to Gil's house."

As I was driving, Curt said he'd seen no point in searching the area; the man had already shown that he was skilled at hiding his tracks. If he found Gil at home, though, he could clear him....

Gil's car was gone. Tacked to the front door, almost as though Curt was expected, was a note written in Gil's huge flowing script: CURT: I HAD TO GO TO K.C. BACK IN A FEW DAYS. GIL.

"That does it," said Curt. "I've got to find out where he is." He turned to me. "You know any of his hangouts, his hotel?"

"He never mentioned any."

"Okay. Now if you'll take us back to town..."

In town Curt said he and Gaby would wait in the car until the station opened and he could get his tires filled. I drove home and crawled into bed as it was getting pink in the east. Lou looked as though he hadn't moved since I left him.

Next morning Gaby came in and asked me to have a Coke with her. I was training a new girl to take Ethel's place, a farm girl named Doris whose husband worked in the grain elevator. I showed her how to use the cash register and joined Gaby in the drug store. We sat at one of the marble-topped ice cream tables which had been there since I was a little girl. Gaby said in a low voice:

"Curt called Kansas City. He's hired a private detective to trace Gil."

Gaby looked tired but no longer frightened, as though she'd gone a step beyond fear. I had an elusive letdown feeling and finally identified it. Since Gaby was telling me this, it meant Curt couldn't see me. Her next words verified it:

"Curt says it isn't safe for you to meet for awhile. He also thinks its better if you don't stay home alone. If your husband isn't there, visit neighbors. Don't let your daughter out alone at night."

"Why is he so worried about me?"

"Not only you. Me too." She jerked her head toward the window. I saw old Tully Robinson and his wife Carrie standing beside Curt's car. They were both Brushcreekers, and I'd known them all my life. Tully had been a brawler in his youth and had once served a term for stealing hogs. Now he was nearly sixty and steadied down. Carrie was a stocky woman with iron-gray hair and biceps as big as Gaby's thighs. She'd been the Nation's midwife for years, but the younger women now used the doctor in

Franklin. She was strong as a man; I remembered seeing her drive mules and strip cane for their sorghum mill. We kids used to eat the sweet sorghum while the foam was still on it. At county fairs Carrie ran the cotton candy concession and Tully the penny-pitch.

"My housekeeper and Curt's hired man," said Gaby. "They're staying with us for a time. Curt says he trusts them implicitly."

"So do I," I said. "But where's Curt?"

Gaby shrugged. "He'll be out of touch until Gil is located. Curt says he's number one suspect." Gaby smiled a bitter smile which did nothing for her beauty. "I liked Gil, but I find myself hoping he's the one. Just to end this damned nightmare."

I looked at Gaby and wondered if I were stronger than she was. I wasn't eager for it to end—perhaps because when it ended, Curt would leave....

CHAPTER FIVE

For a week I had to stay in the store all day while I trained Doris to take over in the afternoons. I didn't see Curt at all, but Gaby came in a couple of times looking pale and Camille-like—particularly alongside ruddy, jovial Carrie Robinson. She'd shake her head when I asked if there was anything new. There was something new, but not in the quest for Gil Sisk. One night a rock smashed the window of Stubb's tavern; attached to it was a printed note saying: THIS IS FOR SANDY BENNETT. Nobody could figure it out except that somebody blamed Stubb because she'd drunk beer there the night she burned. Stubb closed up for a week and went to Excelsior Springs, which contributed to the town's somber aspect. Two mornings later, Bill Struble found a dead dog with its throat cut hanging from the railroad-crossing signal. It was a brindle watchdog—of mongrel breed but mostly boxer—belonging to Fern Blake, the widow of Jerry Blake, who'd been killed when the butane tank blew up in the hardware store. Fern demanded protection, and Sheriff Wade named a special deputy to patrol the area at night. He was Wayne Calvin, a mechanic at Slavitt's auto salvage, Seventh Day Adventist, and about the only unmarried man in Sherman who didn't drink. Tension still mounted; Tillie Sims, 75, who lived alone, saw an eerie face in her window one midnight. Her sister Winifred, 72, who hadn't spoken to Tillie in twenty years, saw a face in her window the following night. The two women moved in together the following day, so it couldn't be said that events were all bad.

The county paper came out that Friday with a three-column headline: PRANKSTER PROWLS SHERMAN.

The story was treated with the Sunday-school type of indignation typical of small-town newspapers. It included a warning from Sheriff Wade that the prankster was guilty of malicious mischief and subject to prosecution.

Just below that story, another tiny headline caught my eye:

CURT FRIEDLAND ARRESTED
RELEASED FOR LACK OF EVIDENCE

Curtis Friedland, former resident of Sherman, was arrested by Sheriff Glen Wade on suspicion of possessing illegal firearms. He was released for lack of evidence.

I pondered the item a minute before I realized it referred to the phony arrest at Curt's place while I watched. Lord! that was how long... over two weeks ago. Two county papers had come out since then.

"Guilt by association," said Curt's voice.

I looked up and saw him standing there. He wore his old denims, but they were deeply wrinkled and stained with red mud, as though he'd been tramping the Brush Creek hills all night. Just seeing him lifted my spirits, but I was depressed by the gray weariness of his face.

"You mean the paper?" I asked.

Curt nodded. "No county sheriff is going to be elected year after year without knowing how to use his local newspaper. He released the story of my arrest knowing the editor usually tries to group all Sherman news together. Most people will just assume that both items were part of the same story. I'm already getting dirty looks."

I folded the paper and shoved it aside. "I've been starving for news, Curt. Haven't you found out *anything?*"

He shook his head. "The detective's looking. I'm looking. Nothing new."

At the same time he was making writing motions with his hand. I slid a pencil and pad over to him and watched him write: *Tomorrow, five p.m. Your mailbox.*

He went out and climbed in his car. I hoped he'd go home and get some sleep.

That night at seven I got a call from Harley Grove, secretary of the town council. He asked me to tell Lou they were having a special meeting of the council. Lou was supposed to come. I asked what it was about; I'd gone to school with Harley and was shocked when he said bluntly: "Council business, Veda. Just tell Lou to be sure and come."

Lou came in at eight and I relayed the message. Then I watched TV without seeing it until Lou came home at ten. He was chuckling as he pulled off his tie. While I mixed him a drink, he said: "They think Curt Friedland's bringing this trouble. They want him pressured out of town."

I felt like I'd been suddenly thrust among foreigners. That's why Harley hadn't told me what the meeting was about. Where had I slipped up? How had word gotten out that Curt and I were... *what did they think we were doing anyway?*

"How could they pressure him?" I asked.

"Someone would talk to him, buy him out. They... had me in mind." He laughed and tipped back his glass. The ice clicked against his teeth. He lowered his glass and belched. "It's the old story of bell-the-cat. Everyone wants the other guy to do it. I told them they'd better forget the idea before it lashes back. Friedland's no hairy-necked Brushcreeker."

I felt grateful to Lou, and guilty because I was working behind his back. But I explained to myself that Lou and I were going through the period of estrangement we usually have when he starts a new project. He was traveling, buying new equipment, supervising the work. I only saw him late in the evenings, and even then he'd usually be working out in the shop, where he'd installed a desk and an adding machine for a makeshift study.

I was watching the mailbox at four-forty p.m. the next day. My heart jumped when I saw Curt's old car stop—but the car drove off immediately. I trudged out and found a brown manila envelope crammed into the box. It contained a book, *The Prophet*, by Kahlil Gibran, and an aerial photo of the Brush Creek wilderness. The book had certain words circled, and the photo was speckled with numbers written in grease pencil. I took it to the house and tried to fathom the connection between the book and the photo. I couldn't. I decided the key was missing. Damn Curt and his penchant for intrigue....

The phone rang at three a.m. I got up, my thoughts suspended. A three a.m. call meant trouble.

"Hello," I said.

"Velda," said a husky, muffled voice. "Listen carefully and you'll know who I am. You got a sandbur in your butt, remember? You didn't notice until you started to pull on your panties, then you had to have him pull it out. You looked funny standing in the gully holding your dress up with your panties down—they were red, I remember the color—while he—"

I slammed down the receiver. My heart was beating so fast I thought it would choke me. Perspiration trickled down my body and between my breasts. My hands were sweaty; I wiped them on my nightgown and felt an urge to scrub my entire body with soap. The words had stained me with filth....

It had been the watcher. No other living person could have known about that embarrassing incident with the sandbur. I walked into the bedroom and looked down at Lou's sleeping figure. I wanted to wake him up, but I'd have to tell him the whole story of Mart and I, about Curt's project—and what could Lou do?

I drank a glass of straight Scotch and felt better. I regretted having slammed down the phone; if I'd listened longer, he might have let slip some clue to his identity. Even now... I lifted the receiver and heard only the crackle and hum of the wires. I called Central and asked: "Did you just put through a call to me?"

"Uh... yes." The operator yawned audibly into the phone. She slept on a couch beside the switchboard. "It came from Connersville I think. Yes. Connersville."

"Thank you. Get me Curt Friedland's residence."

While she was ringing I remembered Curt's warning of secrecy. But it was too late because Gaby was answering, her voice breathless and urgent.

"Is Curt there?"

Gaby sighed. "No. I thought this would be him."

I felt a brief pity for Gaby; in a sense, she was nearer the danger than I was. "I just got a nasty call from... our friend. From Connersville."

"I'll tell Curt when he comes in."

That was all. Next morning in the store I tried by subtle questioning to learn if any Shermanites had been in Connersville the night before. As nearly as I could learn, none had. Gaby came in and we went for another Coke. She said Curt had left for Connersville as soon as he got home. He planned to look for someone from Sherman, especially Gil Sisk. Then she asked: "Did you figure out the code?"

"Not completely. I know the territory in the photo—"

"He thought you would. The page numbers in the book correspond to the numbers on the photo. When he wants to meet you, he'll give you a quote from the book—over the phone or in a note. The page on which the quote appears will be the number of your meeting place. Find the circled word in the phrase, count from the left-hand margin, and you'll have the time of the meeting."

My head was spinning. "Ingenious."

She gave a wry laugh. "He plays it like a chess game. You should see my instructions on what to do in this or that emergency while he's gone. He covers everything but an invasion from Mars." She paused. "The quote for today is: 'Speak to us of love.' "

I frowned. "Don't you know where the place is?"

She shook her head. "No. Nor the time. You see how it works? A person could overhear and still know nothing. Like me." She gave a crooked smile. "He says there's no need to spread the burden of secrecy."

I drove home after work and looked it up. Page eleven. The word "speak" was circled, fourth from the margin. Four o'clock at site eleven. I dressed excitedly in green slacks and sweater; it would be our first meeting in nearly a week.

The site was a cove so choked with cattails that no boat could enter. I sat down on the bank and smoked a cigaret; I was completely hidden from the lake. Cattails arched overhead, a hill sloped up to a deserted farmhouse, and sheep grazed on the hillside. After ten minutes Curt came strolling down the hill; his eyes were puffy and I decided he'd been taking a nap in the farmhouse while he waited for me. He didn't look any more tired than before; maybe he'd reached a level of fatigue where it no longer showed. He sat down beside me and asked me about the call. I told him in general terms, without revealing exactly what Mart and I had been doing there. I tried to describe the voice, but could only say that it was a man's voice, muffled and indistinct. Curt said he'd seen nobody in Connersville, but that a couple of switchboard operators had promised to keep track of calls to Sherman. They might or they might not; at any rate he planned to spend the night there just in case.

Then he fell silent. I still wasn't used to his total lack of small talk. I got nervous. I looked at the hill, the grazing sheep, the blank windows of the farmhouse like staring eye sockets, and I felt a strange emptiness. I had been eager to meet him... now what? I wanted something more, but I knew no way to break through to him... .

Still, it was our daily afternoon meetings which kept me from leaving town. Because the calls continued during the following week. There was no voice; just a ringing late at night, then a hoarse breathing which gave me chills. I'd listen and visualize Curt out patrolling the neighborhood lines. (His listening post at Connersville produced nothing; only the first call had come from there.) Lou would sometimes be in bed asleep and sometimes out in his study working. If he'd asked me about the calls I'd have told him, but he didn't ask. (He wasn't aware of me really. The road job had bogged down; they'd run into rock outcropping and were blasting it out. With each blast Lou's profit margin dwindled.)

Each morning Curt would call with a quotation or else Gaby would bring it into the store. I'd find the spot on the map and Curt and I would meet. Our seventh meeting wasn't much different from any of the others. It took place in a little hickory grove where I'd climbed trees as a girl.

"Another call last night?" asked Curt.

I nodded. "Like the others. He breathed at me. What's new from the detective?"

"On the night of Bernice's death he went to Kansas City, but there's no record of his having stayed in a hotel."

"Maybe he stayed with a woman."

"As a bachelor, why would he hide it?"

I nodded. "True. Gil would be more likely to brag about it."

On the tenth day I said: "Maybe Gil's a victim. He could be lying dead someplace."

Curt nodded. "Sure. The body could be hidden but not the car. The detective has the make and number. Five-thousand dollar convertibles don't sit abandoned for ten days without being noticed." He looked at me sharply. "You have another suspect?"

"I suspect everybody," I said. "I watch the people come in the store and they all act guilty. Sylvester Bloch mumbles to himself all the time. Fred Goff has a twitch in his face. When he looks at me it's like grasshoppers jumping under his skin."

"We've got more than our share of kooks," said Curt. He was whittling a point on a hickory stick. "Maybe it's inbreeding. In my class at school there were fourteen kids, all descended from three couples." He squinted up at the blue sky between the new leaves. "While I went to school with them they were individuals. People. Since I've been away they've become types, like a Washington Irving story of the New England backwoods. Eli Black was Eli Black, boring and stupid at times, but someone to have a certain kind of fun with. Now he fits perfectly the category of a rural loud-mouthed braggart and coward. Marie Herzog was once a moderately attractive, friendly girl, a good dancer, and a girl who'd go all the way in a parked car just to be a good sport. Now she's a frowsy, blowsy, gabbling busybody. Janet was a sharp kid, careful about whom she dated, always on top of the lesson, neat and clean and ready to call attention to the fact that you weren't, but in a good-natured, for-your-own-good manner. She never put out until you'd agreed to go steady. And even then not until you'd hauled her fifty miles to a movie. Now she's a greedy wolfish woman, col-lecting tinsel in that overbuilt house of hers, pushing her husband until the poor bastard's got a crick in his neck from looking over his shoulder to see if she's behind him. She's a Las Vegas type, the kind you see at horse races and in charge of fashion magazines. Rolly Cartwright was a pudgy little guy whose hands were always sweaty, who was always putting the seam of his pants out of the crack of his ass, who giggled in the locker room and seemed to spend a lot of time in the john. Now I can see plain as hell he's a fag. Gloria's a dyke; she stands over there in the post office and she doesn't watch the men go by, she watches the girls. I don't know where or how she gets her kicks now. In high school she was always the girlfriend of the good-looking chick, the one you always had to bring a date for and the guy you brought always said never again. Just when you were going strong with your date in the movies... she'd nudge your date and whisper in her ear. In a restaurant she'd never go to the john unless your date accompanied her, and then in the john she'd try her damndest to screw up your scene, telling your date you'd gotten fresh or something. Well, she's queer. Look at the guy she married, he's just about as effeminate as you can get without being an overt fag. Somebody should do her a big favor, go over and say, Look baby, your scene is women. Stop fighting it and start making it and you'll be a lot happier."

"Why don't you tell her?" I asked.

He shook his head. "No, actually she wouldn't be happier. Guilt would weight her down. She couldn't be a straight dyke; she'd have to tie it up with a little ribbon of social acceptance.... Maybe she and some young chicks could go off to Africa as missionaries...."

"Curt, while you're analyzing—"

He said it before I finished. "What type are you?"

"Yes."

"You've ceased to be a type and become an individual. Everybody does that eventually."

"But you had me typed?"

"Sure."

"Okay. What?"

"Frustrated romantic, good brain but too easily screwed up by emotions—"

"You can stop now."

He grinned. "Don't want to hear?"

"You... go too deeply, Curt. You miss a lot that happens on the surface."

"Eating, sleeping, talking, what else happens on the surface?"

"Well... emotional relationships. Love..."

"Symbolic," he said. "Sublimated narcissism." He got up suddenly, giving me a pat on the hip. "We'd better go."

This was as near as we'd gotten to a personal relationship; we could talk about sex but we couldn't do anything about it. We were as intimate as old lovers, but we'd never been lovers. I suppose that's why it hurt so much when the community turned against me. I was going to work; the morning was clear and sparkling as a diamond, birds twittered, and the air was full of green, growing smells. Suddenly I stopped. Chalked on the sidewalk in front of the bank were the words:

VELDA BAYRD LOVES CURT FRIEDLAND.

My face burned as I scrubbed it out with my foot. Just then I looked through the window of the bank and saw Bob Sieberling, the vice president, polishing his glasses and watching me. There was no friendliness in his look; I knew he'd seen the words and waited for me to come along and rub them out.

That afternoon I told Curt about it. "I felt I didn't know any of those people... Bob Sieberling... the person who wrote the words... I had a feeling they've hated me for years and all their smiles and kind words were faked."

"Did you notice the handwriting?"

"I..." I blushed. "No, I was so embarrassed, I just wanted it erased—"

"Embarrassed of course because it implied you were the aggressor, the brazen hussy pining for unrequited love. If it had said Curt loves Velda you'd have been flattered—"

I swung at him but he ducked. "Be serious. You think it was the killer?"

"Didn't have to be. Once it starts, others will pick it up. As you say, they've been storing it up. Poor little hill girl marries man for money—"

"I *didn't*."

"I'm speaking with the voice of Sherman. Blood will tell, they'll say, and point out that your sister Anne was a naughty girl. Some of them have waited twelve years to say I told you so. I'd say it's only the beginning, Velda."

He was right, because the next day Fern Blake came in and said she'd decided to do her trading in Franklin. She'd never been a very levelheaded woman, and I was cool and polite to her. I simply handed her the bill which had been accruing for ten years. We'd never presented it because her husband had been Lou's partner. I think Fern had some chronic illness; she was a pale, bony-faced woman who wore gloves in the hottest summer. She always dabbed pink rouge high on each cheekbone and smelled as though she'd dumped a whole bag of cheap talcum powder over her body. Her hands shook as she ripped apart the ticket. Her voice trembled as she said:

"Velda, for ten years now I've kept my husband's secret. But I've known, and your nicey-nice ways haven't fooled me. If you bother me with this—"

I could only stare at her. "What... *what* are you talking about?"

"I know. Don't think I don't. Just remember that."

She walked out then, and I remembered.... Lou had wanted to borrow money to go into the turkey business; he'd needed Jerry's signature on his note because there'd be a mortgage on the store. Jerry had come out one night while Lou was attending some meeting in Franklin. (I could never keep track of Lou's organizations.) Sharon was a baby then and in bed, and Jerry pulled a pint bottle out of his inside jacket pocket and said he'd wait for Lou. Jerry was a big, thick-necked redfaced man. He was sweating, and I should have known something was wrong. But the Blakes were family friends; Jerry and Lou owned a boat together and we all four spent weekends on the lake, went bowling together and all that. Jerry and I were on a kidding, platonic basis... I thought. Jerry took a couple of drinks then brought up the note. He didn't think he could sign it. I was surprised, because I'd thought it was all settled. Then I shrugged; it was between him and Lou. Jerry drank twice more from the bottle and said it all depended on me. He had a little cabin on the lake which his wife knew nothing about. If I'd tell him when I could get away he'd give me a key. I didn't intend to torture Jerry; I just couldn't understand. Jerry squirmed and finally blurted out that we could meet there and nobody would ever know. I kept my temper; I stood up and said I was going into the bedroom. If he left immediately I'd keep quiet. If he didn't I'd call either Lou or the sheriff. I left the room and Jerry left the house. How his wife had found out, and how she'd managed to find any implication of misbehavior on my part I didn't know. Jerry had been all bluff anyway; he'd signed the note and I'd seen no sign of friction between him and Lou. Of course, I'd avoided Jerry after that and two years later he died.

I was getting sick of the citizens of Sherman. They were more narrow and bigoted than I'd thought. When I told Curt about it that afternoon he asked: "Did Lou know about it?"

"I never told him."

"Could Blake have told him, or Blake's wife?"

"Why would they, Curt?"

He was silent a moment; we were sitting on a ridge where a tilted rock stratum stuck up like the exposed spine of an ancient dinosaur. I'd picked the year's first bouquet and the flowers were slowly drooping in my hand. Finally Curt gave me a sidelong look: "Not many weeks ago you upheld Jerry Blake as a moral saint. What do you think now?"

"The same thing, I guess. Who knows what I might have done unconsciously to give poor Jerry the idea I was available. He might have thought I was flirting when I was just trying to be friendly."

A faint smile flickered around his mouth. "In other words, it isn't immoral for a man to desire you. Whereas if he desires another woman, as in Gil Sisk's case—"

"Oh Curt! Do you examine your own motives as closely as you do mine?"

He nodded slowly. "Yes. As a matter of fact, I do."

I wanted to ask him then what his motives were toward me. I hadn't been much use to his investigation lately, yet I had a feeling there was something he wanted me to do, something he couldn't ask because he wasn't quite sure of me. . .

Gladys came into the store the next morning and started talking about the days when she was my teacher and had great hopes for me, and how I must realize she was interested only in my own welfare, and finally: "You must know, Velda, you're being talked about."

I felt icy cold. "Am I? Concerning what?"

"You surely know, Velda. Apparently I was mistaken about Curt Friedland. He's just like his brothers."

"You happen to be mistaken about me at this very moment, Gladys."

"Indeed. Why is it that I see you driving west out of town every afternoon?"

Gladys wore a weird smile which revealed the orange-colored gums of her false teeth. Her prominent hooked nose and narrow chin stood out in sharp relief, almost like a parody. "Maybe it's because you're a spying old witch, Gladys."

I regretted the pointless insult at once, but it was too late; Gladys strode out with her head high and I knew that whoever didn't already know my shameful story would hear it before sundown.

I looked out the window; a bleak spring drizzle fell on the street. There'd be no meeting with Curt today. The branches of the elm trees drooped under the weight of moisture and I knew exactly how they felt. I went back into the office with the idea of crying, but even that seemed pointless. I called up Doris and told her I was sick, then I went home and drank beer alone all afternoon.

Next day I noticed a coldness in the people who came in the store. None of the usual gossipy conferences around the cash register; now they talked out on the sidewalk, looking inside occasionally at where I was standing.

There was more than one reason for it. A few had stopped trading in the store and left outstanding bills of nearly two hundred dollars.

My father called me up that night. "Stay away from him, Velda. That family's brought us nothing but grief."

"Suppose Frankie didn't do it?"

"I don't give a damn if he did it or not. She ruined her life chasing that man. He's guilty, one way or another. Let him rot in jail, and keep away from his brother."

He hung up. My father had never been much interested in legal subtleties, but all the same, I was beginning to see what a chunk Curt had bitten off.

The next day my brother stomped in. Gordon and I had always been on good terms; the fact that Anne had been between us in age had saved us from any sibling rivalry. He'd competed with Anne instead of me. But today his face was hard.

"Dad called me last night. I told him I'd go tell Curt Friedland to leave you alone."

I blazed up. "You big helpful oaf. Does it occur to you that I'm thirty-five—?"

"Then go tell him yourself."

"What if I don't want to be left alone?"

"Then you oughta be whipped. Too damn bad your husband is a flatlander or he'd do it himself."

He stomped out the door and got into his car. I stood there a minute, then I realized this was an encounter I couldn't let take place. Curt and my brother fighting... how could anything good come of it?

I locked up the store—business had fallen off anyway—and drove to Curt's as fast as I could. When I got there Curt was sitting on the steps and Gordon was standing. Their poses didn't look belligerent; they weren't even talking about me. They were talking about Anne and Frankie. Gordon was saying:

"...doesn't matter who did what. If he hadn't come back she wouldn't have chased him."

"Gordon," I said. "You can't hold Curt responsible for what his brother did."

Gordon turned to me, but Curt spoke.

"That's the way it works, Velda You know that. I am responsible for what Frankie did. But he didn't do anything." He turned to Gordon. "See if you can answer yes to just one of these questions. Did you ever see Frankie hit a woman? No. Was there any reason why he'd kill Anne? Were they fighting? Was she threatening to leave him? No. In fact, it looked like they were going off together. Somebody didn't like that idea. Somebody else—
"

"Curt, Frankie's lawyer said all this. It didn't save him then, how can it save him now?"

"With proof—"

"Proof! You'll just stir up a stink, I agree with Dad. Let it lay."

"Sure, Gordon. Pretend Frankie's dead. You ever see a prison? Nothing grows around it, no trees, no grass. It's like a poison seeps through the walls and kills all life. Put a man away and forget him. The authorities will take care of him because they're paid to. People outside can assume he's dead; he won't pop up and remind you he's alive. He isn't really. He's got nothing to do in there but watch himself die."

Gordon turned and started away. Curt called after him. "You think he's guilty?"

Gordon shrugged without turning around. "It's out of our hands."

He got in his car and drove away without looking at me. Obviously he'd forgotten what he came for. I looked at Curt. "He planned to warn you away from me. How'd you get him off that?"

"A soft answer turneth away wrath." Curt smiled. "I saw he was mad, but I remembered seeing him in a fight once. You were there. The other guy got him down somehow; you jumped on the guy's back and started pulling his hair and biting and scratching. You were a little savage, all skinny elbows and legs. I didn't want to fight you this morning." He stood up and slid his arm across my shoulders. "Come in. Gaby's got coffee made."

It must have been his fraternal gesture—perhaps his nonchalance—but I suddenly choked up with bitterness. "Curt, listen, if I'm a fool for taking this thing seriously, will you kindly tell me? If it's all a game just... tell me so I can laugh and have a ball too..."

He pulled away and gave me a studied look. "You're really bugged, aren't you?"

"I shouldn't be, I suppose. I'm in trouble with my folks, I've made enemies I didn't want and friends I don't need—"

"You can step out."

"Can I?"

"Sure. Tell them I deceived you. They'll take you back and gladly, because you've done something that makes you interesting. You'll be invited places and women will take you aside to tell you about their affairs so that you'll tell about yours. You'll find life full and complete and with a richness you never dreamed—"

"Oh, shut up." I wasn't mad anymore.

"Seriously."

"Sure. You make the whole community sound like a gabbling chicken coop."

He shrugged. "I see what I see. You want out or not?"

"When I want out I'll get out. I don't need your release."

He smiled, and somehow it all faded away. It always did; you never really came to grips with Curt unless he wanted it that way; it was as though he had spent all his life avoiding traps.

That night, for the first time in weeks, Lou arranged one of his quiet family evenings. He washed the dishes, helped Sharon with her homework, and watched TV. After Sharon had gone to bed, Lou turned off the TV and regarded me with an expression of sadness and pity.

"You know they're talking about you, Velda?"

It was his commiseration which infuriated me; that and the fact that I'd been told so many times.

"How nice," I said. "How utterly suburban."

"You know what they're saying?"

"The worst, I suppose. I'm carrying on shamelessly while you, the faithful husband, slaves away in blind devotion. I'm pregnant with Curt's child, expected to slip off to St. Joe for an abortion at any moment...."

He smiled faintly, and I could see the picture amused him.

"You know," he said, approaching the subject from left field the way he often does, "your family has a strange self-destructive urge. Once a structure shows a few chinks, you yell whoopee, damn the torpedoes, school's out, let's burn the building. Just because one little piece is tarnished, you tear down the whole goddam edifice."

He was talking about our marriage. I didn't want to go into that.

"What are they saying, that I have a weakness for the Friedland family?"

"For violence... destructive men. Maybe you see it in the men, or maybe you bring it out in them, I don't really know."

"Like I bring violence out in you. What a violent man you are, Lou."

A faint smile tugged at the corners of his mouth. "You think so?"

At that moment I didn't know. I said: "You think there's anything in what they're saying about Curt and me?"

"No."

Somehow that only made me angrier. "I see. You are the calm voice of understanding. You only brought it up to remind me of our place in the community, and how we shouldn't do anything to jeopardize our position. I'm expected only to be careful, and if we should decide to sleep together, we should tell you, and you'll make sure that we're discreet about this thing and nobody knows—"

"You can stop now, Velda. Your nose is getting red."

I jumped up and went into the bedroom. While I lay there I could hear him in the kitchen, getting a bottle from the cupboard. I drifted into a half-sleep; I didn't hear him come into the bedroom. Suddenly I felt the blanket jerked off and my nightdress yanked up to my waist. I could hear the rush of breath through his nostrils as his strong hands rolled me and sprawled me on my back. There was no point in pretending to be asleep;

I helped him in order to end it more quickly....

"Every other night, Velda," he said when he rose. "Maybe that will keep you home. That's what all the boys tell me."

Gaby's call awoke me next morning. The eaves still dripped from an early-morning shower. Lou had already left for work and Sharon had gone to the corner to catch the schoolbus. Gaby said:

"Can you come over? It's urgent."

"Has anything happened to Curt?"

"No. One of his traps has sprung. He wants us there. You'll have to come and get me."

She was waiting in front of the house with two suitcases. "He found Gil."

"Found him?" A picture of Gil lying dead in a ditch leaped into my mind, but Gaby's next words corrected it. "He hasn't taken him yet, but he knows where he is. He found out Gil has a cabin on Lake Pillybay. The detective's been watching it. Late last night Gil came back to it. He's still there."

I helped her load the suitcases into my car and asked what they were.

"Recording apparatus," she said. "Just finding the killer won't help Frankie. There has to be a confession, and an impartial witness."

"Who—?"

"You."

As I drove I learned that most of her information had been received in a phone call which instructed her to implement plan 3a. That meant a suspect was cornered and the recording equipment was needed. She showed a sheaf of typewritten pages on which he'd listed plans for various emergencies. One said: *Arrest by sheriff.* It called for Lou to bail him out, and I wondered if Lou really would. Another was labeled: *My death. Clear out without delay. Hand evidence to FBI and forget* it. That one horrified me; I knew Curt thought that way, but seeing it coldly written on paper made it seem almost as though it had already happened.

Gaby directed me to the opposite side of Lake Pillybay, a rolling wooded area which Shermanites seldom visited. Curt was waiting at a crossroads; he looked pale and grim and he wasted no breath saying hello.

"Cabin's down there. Detective Boggus is watching it. You two wait here until I get this stuff strung out."

He took the two suitcases and disappeared into the dripping woods. After a half hour he came back.

"Okay. We'll go in close."

We got out of the car and closed the doors silently. We started down the dirt road; I was too tense to ask questions. Suddenly Curt stopped and motioned us close:

"The cabin's right around this bend. You two go in there—" he pointed to a break in the sumac which lined the road "—and hide where you can see the action. I'll knock on the door and see if I can startle Gil into making a move."

Gaby motioned me to go first; I guess she assumed I was an experienced woods-runner. We crawled through the underbrush; each time I brushed against a sapling it dumped a shower of droplets on me. We were both soaked by the time we came in view of the cabin. It was a sprawling lodge with a green roof and brown siding. The forest surrounded it from three sides, making it a perfect hidden love nest. I wondered how many Sherman women knew the inside of it; I wondered who Gil had with him now. There was no sound; the only sign of occupancy was Gil's convertible standing just outside the door.

I saw Curt walking toward the door, his shoes squishing in the mud. He knocked loudly and waited, his eyes roving the woods. They passed ever us without pause, so I decided we were well hidden.

After a moment Gil opened the door. His eyes widened at the sight of Curt; he stepped out quickly and jerked the door shut behind him. His hairy shanks protruded from beneath a maroon silk bathrobe. He stood blinking in the light, looking rather more embarrassed than scared. His face looked stiff and painted, like a theatrical mask. I couldn't hear the conversation, but Curt obviously wanted to go inside and Gil didn't want him to. Finally Curt squared his shoulders as though he were about to shove Gil aside and open the door. Gil shrugged; he opened the door and called out a name. It sounded like "Bunny" but it must have been "Benny" because a young man appeared in the door. He looked slim and girlish, with long hair and a narrow, large-eyed face which also had a painted look. He frowned at Curt and pouted his full red lips. Curt turned abruptly and started walking away. Puzzled, I heard Gil call out in a plaintive tone which didn't sound like Gil's voice.

"Say, old fellow, you don't plan to noise this around Sherman, do you?"

"No," said Curt gruffly, "I won't."

Gil slid his arm around the boy's shoulders and the two went inside. Their attitudes were those of a husband and wife who'd just gotten rid of an unwelcome visitor and abruptly I understood. My face prickled with embarrassment, whether for Gil or Curt or just for the human condition, I wasn't sure. I looked into Gaby's wide eyes and saw that she understood it too.

At the car, Curt discharged Detective Boggus with a check; he was a short, chubby man with a dozen black hairs combed carefully over a bald pate, not at all my idea of a private detective. Curt loaded the recording equipment in his car—telling Gaby to erase it, since it was useless, and to drive on home. "I'll ride back with Velda," he said.

For a time we drove in silence, then he said: "You understood the scene back there?"

"Yes."

"How do you feel about Gil?"

I had to think, because I'd identified so closely with Curt that I'd felt only disappointment at the failure of his trap. "About Gil? I think... all that muscle, manhood... what a terrible waste."

He laughed abruptly. "That's funny as hell. I've heard men say exactly the same thing about an attractive Lesbian." He sobered abruptly. "But that explains Gil's absences... and why he worked so hard to get a reputation as a ladies' man. I'll have to take him off the list for good. That kid was wearing lipstick; Gil had it smeared all over his face. You wouldn't fake that." He grimaced. "Stop here. I need a drink."

It was a little gas station and honky-tonk; the kind you see around the country with names like Burntwood Inn and Cozy Dell. This one was called Pine Cove Tavern and was crowded (there was no work in the fields because of the rain) with men in overalls and a couple of women in print dresses. We drew stares as we walked to a booth in the back. I felt wicked and daring, and though it was unlikely that any Shermanites would see me, I found that I didn't really care if they did. I told Curt to order me a boilermaker: a glass of beer with a shot of bourbon inside it. He ordered the same for himself and drank silently for a few minutes. Finally he said: "You've been patient, Velda, working in the dark. Now I'll tell you something, but I've got to have your word you'll keep the secret."

"Okay. You've got it."

"Specifically, I want you not to tell Lou."

I stared at him. I was mad at Lou at the moment, but I didn't like the position I was being put in. "I don't know if I should promise that, Curt."

He shrugged and drank his drink. He wasn't going to tell. Finally I asked: "Does it concern Lou?"

"Yes."

"And me?"

"Yes."

"Then you've got to tell me."

"Promise first."

"Curt, I'll throw this beer in your face."

"Go ahead."

"Look, does it... I mean, if I don't tell Lou, will it get him into trouble?"

"No."

"He won't suffer?"

"The incident is done and past. If it were known in Sherman, people might smile, but nobody would blame him. It will only add to your fund of knowledge concerning your husband, but nothing which will work to your advantage."

"God, I've got to know. I promise not to tell Lou."

"Okay. Remember that night you met me in the store, and I searched for hidden microphones?"

"Yes."

"Lou followed you."

I gasped. "No!"

"I watched after you went in, remember? He drove his pickup past the head of the alley and parked somewhere. Later he came back and stood in the shadows. He didn't see me watching him."

"You didn't say anything then."

"I was waiting to see what he'd do."

"He didn't let the air out of your tires?"

"No. He was there all the time. When Gaby honked, he disappeared."

I felt angry and prickly. "Damn him. Of all the sneaky..." I looked at Curt, who was smiling. "Why did you tell me this now?"

"I need some information from you."

I looked down at my drink. I felt depressed. "About Lou?"

"Yes."

I shook my head. "If you suspect Lou you... you're crazy. He was in bed when the phone calls came. He was home the night that Sandy was killed. He was in Omaha when my sister Anne was killed. He was in the alley the night the air was let out of your tires—"

He was nodding. "I know all that, Velda. But he's a common denominator. He was Jerry Blake's partner, and Jerry Blake made a pass at you. To a jealous man that's a motive for murder right there...."

"He isn't jealous. And he didn't *know.*"

"We aren't sure. Even if he didn't he profited by Jerry's death. He took over the store; he had partner's insurance on Jerry and he collected that. And when Ethel's husband died he bought another store cheap. I don't know his relationship to Anne, but there was Mart. He married you when Mart was killed—"

"Curt, I won't listen to another word."

"All right, let me put it another way. When Gil Sisk faded out as a suspect, it left me with nothing"

"Johnny Drew."

"Okay, Johnny Drew. Anne was about to leave him, that's a possible motive for killing her. But how can you tie him with the others?"

"He worked for Jerry Blake and Jerry fired him. Okay? And Mart... I don't know. Once Johnny said he'd been in love with me all his life. That could have been drunk talk, or it could have been true. There's something else. Johnny gambled a lot, and sometimes he was terribly lucky. Once he took Anne to Bermuda on his winnings. She came back alone, wired home for money because he'd lost again. He used to disappear after he'd make a killing. People figured he was living up his winnings, but who knows? To me he's a prime suspect."

"Okay. But he's disappeared."

"Find him."

"I will, but I need some more help. Your husband's a smart man, probably smarter than you think. I could use his help. If I clear him I can trust him."

"Is that why you've been playing games with me? Waiting until I was ready to spy on my husband?"

"Spy?" He looked thoughtful. "Okay, call it spying if you like."

I had a giddy sensation which didn't come from the liquor I'd drunk. I'd just looked into myself and it was like looking down a deep well; I found to my surprise that Curt had timed me perfectly, because I was ready.

"What do you want to know about Lou" I asked.

"Everything," he said. "Everything you know."

Chapter Six

When I told Curt about Lou, I told myself I was simply laying to rest Curt's suspicions about him. But I suppose it was partly to examine my own feelings about Lou. It's hard to explain my motives; it was like two radio programs going at once, each drowning out the other.

Lou came from a small town near Connersville. He used to visit his aunt here during the summers. He played with the Brush Creek boys: Eli Black, Rolly Cartwright, Mart and Gil and Johnny Drew and Frankie and Teddy Groner who'd drowned, but he'd been gone every winter and he never really belonged. He seemed to endure an initiation every spring when he'd come to visit his aunt. She was a fanatical Methodist, and each summer she'd launch Lou's visit by trying to indoctrinate him into the church. I remember seeing Lou in the churchyard in necktie and shiny patent leather shoes wearing a frozen smile while the boys ran up to spit on the shoes. After a few weeks, Lou's aunt would drop the church routine, but Lou never completely made it with the boys. During the war he was 4-F because of a heart murmur and that cut him off even further. He came to Sherman to run his aunt's farm, then he ran Jerry Blake's store when Jerry joined the Navy. Lou started making money, and people resented that. One fight I remember . . not really a fight—with Johnny Drew.

"What happened?" asked Curt.

"It was at Gable's tavern where the Brushcreekers went—the quiet drinkers used the other one. I was fourteen then, and I'd gone in to see Dad—on Saturday night he'd drink beer and I could figure him for a dime provided I got there before my brother and sister had cleaned him out. I used to hang around awhile; it was an exciting place, always a few servicemen, loud talk and sometimes a fight. On this night Lou was sitting at the bar drinking a beer. I didn't notice him until Johnny Drew came in. He was just out of boot camp, wearing his marine dress uniform with marksmanship medals all over it. He saw Lou in civvies and decided to have some fun. He said, 'What's wrong, Lou? You have an eardrum punctured?' Lou murmured something which nobody else heard, and Johnny said: 'I don't see how that could keep you from fighting.' 'Well, the Army thought so,' said Lou. And Johnny said: 'It couldn't keep you from stepping over into the park and having a friendly little match?' Lou said he'd rather drink his beer. Johnny turned to the crowd and said: 'Whaddaya think, this civilian would rather drink his beer.' Then he laughed and knocked the beer in Lou's lap. Everyone got quiet waiting to see what Lou would do.

He reached in his pocket and pulled out a knife. The blade wasn't more than two inches long, but the quiet way he did it, kind of sad and regretful, caught everybody's attention. He jabbed it into the bar in front of him and ordered another beer. He didn't even look at Johnny, but Johnny got the message. He walked out and never bothered Lou again. That's the way Lou worked; I've never seen him lose his temper. It's like something he keeps in a bottle and lets loose only when it will do some good."

"Yes," said Curt. "He's a rich man now."

"Well, he made it honestly. He started with the farm his aunt left him, then bought into the hardware store when Jerry came back from the Navy. He had a talent for being in the right place at the right time. Take the turkeys... when the big feed companies started offering inducements to get people to raise turkeys, Lou borrowed money to get into it: ten thousand poults the first year, fifty thousand the next, a hundred thousand the year after that. Suddenly the whole county was raising turkeys, and Lou stepped out. That year the bottom dropped out of the turkey market and those who were still in lost their shirts. Not Lou. And construction.... when the government started subsidizing farm ponds, Lou bought a bulldozer and started digging. Everybody wanted work done; things had fallen apart during the war and everybody was rolling up their sleeves to put it back in shape. Lou bought more equipment; he built roads and reservoirs and a string of small airfields to get ready for the big air age. The air age never panned out. You can see some of the fields be built, weeds coming up around the concrete, a ramshackle hangar, a couple of peeling piper cubs. Some people went broke, but not Lou. He'd taken his profit and gone on to something else. Somehow he knew when to get in and when to get out. The fact that he happened to make money when certain people died means nothing. He made money at everything."

As we were driving home, Curt asked: "How about Mart's death."

I thought about it. "Lou took me out a few times while Mart was in the service, but he didn't seem serious. Never really tried anything beyond a single goodnight kiss when he took me home. I was going to marry Mart, and he seemed to accept it. In fact, he sold Mart the farm we planned to live on after we were married. When Mart died Lou took me to the scene of the accident and showed me that he'd bulldozed off the bank so that no more accidents could happen."

"And just happened to cover up the evidence," said Curt. "I wonder who told Struble he should have the well filled in."

My face felt hot. "You're twisting everything up, Curt. Lou just gets a kick out of helping people behind the scenes. Like the sheriff. . ."

"He helped the sheriff?"

"Loaned him money or something. I don't know."

"And I suppose the sheriff shows his gratitude."

"Well... not directly. When somebody in Sherman has trouble they often ask Lou to smooth things over with the sheriff. Like Johnny Drew when he passed some bad checks—"

"What did Lou get out of that?"

"Nothing, for Pete's sake. Maybe a feeling of importance, I don't know. Curt, don't get me started looking at motives. I have to look at what a man *does*. Lou showed up pretty good after Anne's death. My folks never had any other home, but here they were surrounded by painful memories. Lou had a farm fifty miles away and he made Dad a proposition; he could live on the place for life and give him a tenth of the crop. It was twice as good a farm as the one they had here."

"Are they happy there?" asked Curt.

"Are you looking for trouble?"

"No, but people uprooted at that age—"

"Maybe they'll adapt. They don't like it there, but who knows whether they'd like it here or not?"

"Why'd he pick a farm so far away?"

I realized that everything I said in defense of Lou could be turned against him. Curt could have said that Lou wanted my folks out of the way so that Anne's murder would be forgotten. I didn't believe him.

But that evening I looked at Lou sitting under the reading lamp and realized that I had no idea of what went on in his head. He *could* kill; any man could kill if he thought he had to. Our country's wars have taught us that if nothing else. I thought of Lou creeping up while I slept; I damned Curt for planting this little seed of horror....

Next day Curt wanted me to take him to see Lou's mother. I wondered how I'd explain the visit, but I needn't have worried. Lonely old women don't question the rare arrival of visitors. Lou's mother was a starchy white-haired woman living in a prim white house on an elm-shaded street.

She told Curt what a well-behaved boy Lou had been; always went to church, always did his homework. I'd heard it all before, so I concentrated on stifling yawns until she displayed some relics of Lou's eight-year-old interest in taxidermy: twenty little white mice, almost perfectly preserved.

Curt looked at me and smiled; I wondered what his suspicious mind was making of this. Personally, it made me realize what a strange, lonely childhood Lou had had.

That night I talked to Lou about Bernice Struble. I told myself I was personally curious, but I'd reached the point of not being sure whose motives I was acting on, my own... or Curt's. Lou didn't seem interested in the subject but said yes, he'd told Struble the well would have to be filled.

"You wouldn't expect people to drink out of it. Would you, Velda?"

I had to admit that I wouldn't.

The next night I was surprised to see Curt's old car coming up the drive. Curt and Gaby stepped out dressed for visiting, Curt in slacks and knit shirt, Gaby in a wraparound skirt and blouse. I met them at the gate and my face must have revealed worry because Curt said: "Just a social call. Relax."

I didn't relax, because I knew Curt had come to study Lou. I must admit that Lou seemed pleased to see them; he kept the glasses filled and led the conversation.. I found that I wasn't the only one on edge. Gaby was watching Curt and acting on his signals. She'd reach for a third drink and abruptly refuse it; she'd start telling a story and suddenly change the subject. I began picking up his signals; a slight pinching of the lips and a movement of the eyes. Lou missed them, I'm sure. I saw them because Curt didn't try to hide them from me.

Maybe it was curiosity, but I didn't want to leave Curt and Lou alone. When Lou took him out to see the shop, I went along. It was weird to hear Curt lead the conversation into the subject of wire taps and hidden receivers: "With transistors and printed circuits," said Curt, "you could hide a receiver in a cigaret lighter. If somebody wanted to spy on you, you'd never be out of earshot."

When Lou showed Curt his guns, Curt asked questions and showed polite interest, but it was clear to me that he was studying Lou and not the guns. I'd always felt that Lou bought guns just for the joy of possession, but Curt led the conversation to killing. "I don't like guns particularly. As tools for killing they're so damned... noisy. If I were going to kill a man I'd never use a gun."

"What would you use?" asked Lou.

Curt smiled. "That would depend on the situation. I'd kill a man only if he were trying to kill me, and then I'd use... whatever I had."

"You might happen to have a gun," said Lou.

"If I did, it would be because I expected to need it. And if I expected to need it, I might create a situation where I did. The subconscious plays funny tricks."

Lou nodded, but I was puzzled by Curt. It seemed to me that if Lou *were* the killer, he would *know* that Curt suspected him. Then I remembered: Curt wanted the killer to make a try at him.

Later they talked about the killing instinct; I don't know who led the conversation into it, Curt or Lou, but suddenly Lou was saying he'd never been in the service so he didn't know if he could kill or not. He'd always been awed by the way the Army made killers out of ordinary farm boys-

—

Curt shook his head. "They- don't *create* killers, Lou, they educate the one that every man has inside him."

Lou raised his brows. "Seems like a risky business. They can't be sure they've got him de-educated. One minute the killer's a patriotic citizen; suddenly there's an armistice and the killer becomes an antisocial beast."

Gaby laughed. "You should get Curt to show you the psychiatric study they did on him. They didn't think they could get him to stop."

"Stop what?" I asked.

"Stop kill—uh, fighting."

An awkward silence fell in the room. Gaby drew back in her chair and I think she regretted her words because the psychiatric study was obviously a touchy subject with Curt. But it was out and he had to deal with it.

"They gave me a clean bill," he said. "I got an honorable discharge, finally. But like you said Lou, I resented those bastards in Washington who think they can turn a man into a killer by pushing a button that says go. Then turn him into a decent taxpayer by pushing one that says stop. I wanted to show them that I controlled my own switch. So I let the fighting machine run on a little while until they got panicky, then I got tired of the game. I shut myself off." He rose from his chair and walked to the table, poured his glass full of straight bourbon. He looked at me over the rim and for a second there was something in his eyes I didn't like. Then he went on: "For a while it would get turned on again without warning. Other guys could turn it on, but only I could shut it off." You'd never know Curt was excited, except that between each sentence he'd drink. I found myself sitting on the edge of my chair. "Now I control both ends," he said, taking a drink. "I turn it on." Drink. "I shut it off." Drink. "It's a comforting feeling to control your own killer. Everybody should do it." Drink. "But to do it you have to let him run loose until you know him well enough to get a halter on him. Takes a war to do it, Lou. That's where you're at a disadvantage."

He smiled, set his empty glass down on the table, and walked back to his chair. I felt an immense relief, because I felt he'd re-experienced the entire war while he was talking to us. I resolved never again to ask him about the Army or the war because of the way his eyes went flat and dead....

I glanced over at Lou and saw a studious look in his eyes. I realized that just for a minute they'd switched roles; Lou was the observer, and Curt was the subject. . .

After they'd gone Lou sat with an untouched drink in his hand looking at the empty TV screen. I showered and dressed for bed; as I passed Lou's chair he asked without looking up:

"What do you think of him?"

I paused. "He's like you, Lou, in certain ways."

Lou jerked his head up. "How so?"

I sat down on the hassock and tried to define my vague feelings. "I don't mean physically. You're opposites there; he's tall and blond, you're short and dark. But you have the same way of talking, those long rushing declarations when nobody can get a word in edgewise. And you both have an uncanny way of shifting the burden of proof to the other person. You get the other person talking, explaining, apologizing, then suddenly the guy gets a puzzled look in his eyes and wonders why he's apologizing...."

When I paused, Lou said: "Go on."

"Well, neither of you seem to have close men friends. You think weird thoughts, all that talk of death and killing. You don't tell jokes. You don't *enjoy* things... at least not the way I see enjoyment. I don't understand what goes on inside either of you, only the parts you let show above the surface. But Curt seems... tighter, somehow. He cares more about things... doesn't dissemble quite as well...."

Lou smiled vaguely. "He's nine years younger. Give him time."

The meaning of that burst on me suddenly: I thought, my God, Curt is nine years younger than Lou. I'd actually considered them the same age, and I thought: If they're even now, where will Curt be when he's Lou's age? At that moment I regretted that I wouldn't be there to see it, because I felt that he'd leave me far behind.

Lou's curiosity was engaged, and the next night he took me to see Curt and Gaby. There was a farmhouse near Curt's—Lou had the place listed for sale—where the attic was full of bats. Lou liked to sit and shoot them as they darted out at sunset. It was like a skeet shoot, only trickier. Curt was reluctant to do it, and I thought he was squeamish. But Lou insisted, and Curt took the gun. Bang, he took one shot and got one bat. Then he handed Lou the gun and said: "That's all. I won't push my luck." Lou took five more shots and only winged one. When all the bats had flown, Curt said he thought he'd go up and board up the hole, but Lou said: "Leave it open. They'll come back."

Curt smiled and said. "I see. Then we'll have more to shoot tomorrow."

I'd never thought of it like that but Lou's deal with the bats seemed suddenly sadistic and perverted. Before it had seemed like harmless fun.

Afterward Lou said: "He doesn't like killing, you notice that? He just likes talking about it."

I looked at Lou. "*Should* a person like it?"

"No, certainly not." Lou chuckled to himself; he seemed oddly self-satisfied.

I felt uncomfortable watching the two together, each studying the other. Occasionally I'd pick up fragments of weird conversation. Curt saying: "Life is telling yourself a break will come, tomorrow will be better. Suicide is deciding it won't come, or if it does it won't be worth a damn." And Lou asking: "Suppose you decided, how would you do it?" Curt said: "I'd choose to wait for death from some outside agency. Then each day would be profit, reckoned from the day I decided." Lou laughed. "It's altogether too sane.

When you really decide on suicide, you're nuts. Right now you're sane, so you plan simple painless methods. But if you ever really do it, you'll be kooky, so naturally your methods will be kooky too." "Yes," Curt agreed finally. "And you'll probably take a few people with you."

A week passed; Lou spent less time at his work and no longer puttered in his shop at night. I was torn between worry and willingness to see Curt under any circumstances. Lou would get in the car in the evenings and say, Well, shall we go to a show or what? And I'd say, Whatever you want, Lou. And my stomach would knot up because tonight I wouldn't see Curt, then Lou would say, Shall we stop and see Curt and Gaby? And my tongue would stick to the roof of my mouth because I knew before the evening was over Curt and Lou would be sizing each other up, like a pair of tomcats. Everything was a kind of contest, like the water skiing. Lou had been skiing for years and was far better than average. He asked Curt if he'd ever skied, and Curt said: "I've tried a couple of times." From then on Lou couldn't rest until he got him on a pair of boards. I stood on the bank and watched his first wobbly, wallowing attempts. An hour later I watched his smooth gliding ease; a day later I saw him slalom and carry Sharon on his back. Lou strained to stay ahead of him, but I could see it was useless. Then, just when Lou and Curt were exactly equal in skill, Curt said: "I'm beginning to lose interest in the sport."

I thought about that. I realized that if he'd gone on to surpass Lou, I might have pitied Lou and resented Curt. But when he didn't go ahead, he got all the credit and none of the blame. He was as superior physically as if he had, yet he didn't have to bear the burden of having put Lou down.

I still hadn't figured it out completely, though. One afternoon we were shooting the basketball at the net Lou had tacked onto the garage for Sharon. Curt dropped ten in a row which just whispered through the net. He seemed to forget the rest of us were there; we were just co-spectators in his drive to attain perfection. Then he seemed to remember that we were keeping score; he started clowning and missing shots. Lou beat him, but everybody knew Curt could have won. I had a feeling Curt was trying to infuriate Lou, in a way which left Lou no excuse to be angry. Curt was so blithe and easy about it, the way he shot the arrows. Lou got pretty good with the bow, but never as good as Curt—and Curt was always ready with a lame, unhelpful excuse:

"Your arms are too short; you need a lighter bow." I felt like screaming at Lou, For God's sake get off the physical kick; you're just playing into his hands. But Lou didn't seem to notice; trying the tablecloth trick was his own idea. Curt watched Lou do it twice, breaking a plate and two glasses. Then he walked to the table and jerked off the cloth with one hand. He didn't even ripple the cream in the pitcher. He treated it as an accident and wouldn't try it again; but I knew that somehow Curt had practiced, then had worked Lou into trying it first. When we were alone I asked: "Are you always on top?"

He smiled. ""There are better men. I met them back in the days when I was trying everybody out."

"That must have shocked you."

"It was a sobering lesson. It taught me never to deceive myself."

I couldn't figure out Curt's game with Lou. I wondered if *he* knew; I felt that we were all four in a driverless car hurtling downhill toward certain disaster.

Gaby felt it too; she got a bright nervous glitter in her eyes. Her checks grew hollow and she cursed the town: "Goddam dusty stinking little pig-pen." I suspected she was hitting the bottle secretly, but she kept it all from Curt. She made me promise not to tell, then told me she'd gotten nasty phone calls at the same time I'd been getting them.

"Why didn't you tell Curt?" I asked.

"I was supposed to," she said. "I was supposed to rave and scream and get scared so Curt would pull out. That's why I didn't."

I had to admire her courage; slim, elfin creature. She'd never really had her nose rubbed against life before. She couldn't have been more than twenty-five. I felt sorry for her, but at the same time envious, watching her and Curt together. I saw him kiss her in the car, and I tried to remember how long it had been since Lou and I had done that. When we'd leave their house, they'd stand on the front porch together and Curt would slide his arm across her shoulders. There was something basic about that; a gesture of solidarity in front of the home which hints that everything's good inside.... When they left our house, I always walked Curt to the car, and Lou walked with Gaby. I'd make these comparisons and I'd feel a prickle of discontent.

One day Sharon came to me with a problem. It was Sunday; Lou and Gaby were out riding, Curt and I were sitting on the blanket in front of our house. Sharon had been told by a boy she liked that he preferred short hair. Sharon wanted to know, Should I cut it, or would that make me seem too eager?

I said: "Well, I'm not a boy. Why don't you ask Curt?"

Curt looked at me curiously, then at Sharon: "I'm afraid I didn't have a normal boyhood. Why don't you ask your dad?"

She left to do that, and Curt kept looking at me. Finally he said quietly: "He's her dad, and nothing I do will change that. I don't tamper with things I can't change."

"I know." I felt everything coming down on top of me, covering me with confusion. I jumped up. "I know he's her dad, and I know he loves her. And she loves him. I just wish there were more understanding between them and less emotion. I wish you were—" I turned away suddenly, my face burning. "My God, this thing is getting out of control."

He shook his head. "No, it isn't."

"But... it has. You've gotten so involved in your little game with Lou you've forgotten—"

"It's all one game, Velda."

I stared at him. "But I thought by now you'd clear him—"

"On the contrary. I've noticed that the phone calls have stopped since I've been staying close to Lou."

My mind started spinning. I couldn't put two thoughts together. "Then... how can you leave Gaby alone with him so much?"

"I'm usually within calling distance."

"Not now. They've been gone an hour on the horses."

He nodded. "I know. Put your ear to the ground."

I lay my ear against the ground and heard the faint thudding of hoofs. I looked at Curt. "What would you do if they stopped?"

"Go find them," he shrugged. "But it isn't necessary now. Sharon went for me."

It made me furious that he'd used my daughter. "Damn you. You treat everybody like bugs under a glass."

He reached up and took my hand. I looked into his eyes and saw that the pupils were large and black, with only tiny rims of blue around them. "Hold yourself together, Velda. Something's going to break soon."

I hoped so. I was tired of lying in bed every night and adding up the score: This counted for Lou, that counted against him. Was he, or wasn't he? I'd added it a hundred times and never got enough on either side to settle the account. I doubted that any wife had ever been faced by such a problem.

The following night all my suspicions of Lou were wiped out. It was ten o'clock. Lou was out in the shop; Gaby and Curt had just left, and I was sitting with one eye on the TV and the other eye on the clock. Sharon had ridden the gelding to visit a girlfriend who lived two miles up the road; I'd been against letting her go, but Lou and Sharon had both opposed me, so I'd given in.

The phone rang, a hesitant ring which told me it was being cranked manually and not by the switchboard, which has a push button. That meant a call from somebody on our line. Since those weird calls had always come on our line, I lifted the phone fearfully.

"Mrs. Bayrd," said a woman's voice. "This is Crystal Miller. Can you come up? Your daughter's here."

My heart stopped. The Millers lived just a half mile up the road. "Is Sharon hurt?"

"She's... not hurt, but—" She started to say more but stopped. "You'd better come right away. That's all I can say."

I ran out the door and called to Lou. The door opened, and he was silhouetted by the light behind him. "Lou! Sharon's up at Miller's! Something's happened!"

We wheeled into the Millers' lane and stopped; Bert Miller came out of the square white house and sauntered down to meet us. He was a retired railroader who wore greasy overalls and smoked a corncob pipe which was unbearably rancid even if you liked pipes—which his wife didn't. "She's inside," he drawled as though this were a social visit. "I don't think you folks need to worry. Some kids threw a scare into her, I figure. I found her hammerin' at my door, her shirt half torn off. She was bawlin'..."

Lou strode past him toward the house, then Bert said: "I called the sheriff; he's on his way."

Lou paused in midstride, then nodded abruptly and went on. I walked behind him, into a neat living room which smelled of waxed linoleum and sassafras tea. The sassafras wafted up from a glass in Sharon's hand. She sat in an armchair, pale and puffy-eyed, wrapped in a large plaid bathrobe. Crystal Miller stood behind her with bony arms folded across her chest, her pale gray eyes fixed on me.

"You shouldn't let your daughter out at night, Mrs. Bayrd, with all those strange things happening."

I ignored her and went to Sharon. "What happened, baby?"

Sharon took a deep breath and blurted: "I was riding Lightning down the road and a bright light flashed and Lightning jumped and I fell, and—"

She stopped abruptly. "Go on, Sharon," I said.

"Don't rush her, Velda," said Lou. "Just tell the story, Sharon. No hurry now."

Sharon looked down at the tea. Tears started running down her cheeks. "Mother . . . I can't drink this."

I took the tea and handed it to Crystal Miller. Her lips pursed with disapproval, but she took it.

Bert Miller said: "A shot of whisky would—"

"Shut up, Bert," snapped his wife.

"Go on, Sharon," I said.

"Well... I lay in the road with the breath knocked out of me. Then something... ran over from the side of the road, growling like an animal."

"A dog?"

"Oh *no*. It was a man, I know that, but the sound was like an animal. It started tearing at my clothes... my shirt. I started kicking and screaming, and it was tearing at my Levis... but all of a sudden it ran away."

"Ran away?"

"I guess my screaming scared it off."

"But... he didn't do anything?"

"Yes he *did*, Mother. He tore off my shirt and ripped my jeans—"

"But he just ripped them? He didn't... I mean afterwards—"

"Oh, Mother!" Sharon started sobbing.

"Velda," said Lou. "You're not getting through." He came forward and helped Sharon out of her chair. "Let's go in the other room and talk."

The door closed behind them and I heard Lou's soothing voice. After a minute Bert Miller cleared his throat and said if I could use a drink, he'd just walk out to the barn. But Crystal told him to shut up, she wouldn't have the stuff in the house; Bert shrugged and we sat in awkward silence for five more minutes. A car purred to a stop outside, then the sheriff came in, bulking huge in creased gabardines. He pulled off his hat and said: "Hello folks, Velda. Where's the girl?"

Lou and Sharon came out, Lou with his arm around Sharon's waist. He said: "Sorry you got called out on a wild goose chase, Sheriff. The girl just fell off her horse."

I stared at Lou. The sheriff said: "Hell! I heard she got raped."

Lou turned to Sharon. "Baby, tell the sheriff what happened."

"I..." Her voice was husky from crying. "I fell off the horse and tried to catch him and tore my clothes in the fence."

I gasped. "Sharon! Why did you tell that story?"

She looked down, refusing to meet my eyes. "Because... I'd stayed longer than you said, I didn't want to be punished."

"But I never... you knew you wouldn't be—"

The sheriff cleared his throat. "I'll be getting back, unless..." he looked at Lou "...you think I ought to look into it?"

Lou shook his head. "No, I'm sure it happened like she said."

I watched the sheriff leave, too dazed by events to say anything. Lou drove the pickup out of the lane, with Sharon sitting between us. On the road he stopped and said: "Drive on home. I'll check the area for tracks."

I stared at him. "You mean... her story was true?"

"Yes."

My mind buzzed in total confusion. "You mean you covered it up to keep it out of the paper? You think your standing in the damn community is more important than our daughter, for *God's sake?*"

Lou sighed. "Velda, I know exactly what I'm doing. You remember the Covin girl? It damn near ruined her life when they took that boy to court for raping her."

"But the sheriff could have helped quietly—"

"Don't argue, Velda. Take Sharon home and put her to bed."

He slammed the door and walked down the road. I drove Sharon home and drew a hot bath for her. As I bathed her, I saw that the struggle had been far more violent than she'd led me to believe. There were bruises on her breasts and neck. My throat ached when I saw the finger marks on the lower curve of her stomach. He'd reached down, grabbing for the soft tender womanhood. I felt prickly and nervous handling her body; the child seemed suddenly to have become a woman, full-breasted and fledged and desired by men—so desired that they used force to take what they wanted. I thought to myself: *It may be a game for Curt, but it's no longer a game for me.*

As I tucked Sharon in bed, I asked: "You know what he was trying to do?"

"Mother, of course. I'm fifteen."

I wondered how she knew—then I recalled that I had known when I was fifteen, but couldn't say how I knew.

"He didn't do it though? You're sure?"

"I'm sure. It was the Levis. He couldn't tear them, and I kept my legs crossed."

I heard the door slam. I said goodnight to Sharon and left her. Lou said he'd found signs of a scuffle on the gravel and a button off her shirt. But there'd been no tracks on the gravel and none on the shoulder. He said goodnight to Sharon, then fixed a drink and sat down.

"Velda," be said heavily, "it's time we had a talk about this investigation of Curt's."

"He told you about it?"

Lou shook his bead. "I've watched it in operation, Velda. You can't dissemble as well as you imagine. Go ahead, call him up. I think he'll be ready to talk."

Curt asked a hundred questions about Sharon—exact time, location... so on... but I couldn't say much on the phone. Lou's eyes were on me constantly. At last Curt said he'd be over as soon as be could. When I hung up Lou said:

"He doesn't trust anybody, does he?"

"He's coming," I said.

I dreaded the next few hours: all the days Curt and Lou had been together I'd felt they were building up to some kind of ultimate encounter. I was afraid it might come tonight and I had a feeling they were too evenly matched to do anything but destroy each other. I watched Lou setting out glasses and putting ice cubes in a bowl as though it would be a social gathering; he seemed strangely exhilarated in view of what had happened to Sharon. I discovered that my underclothes were damp with perspiration; I took a shower and put on clean clothes. When I came out of the bedroom, Curt and Gaby were there. Lou was reading from Curt's list of accidents, sipping his drink from time to time.

Curt sprawled in an armchair with his heels on the floor in front of him, holding his glass with both hands and peering at the light through the liquor. Gaby was smoking, rolling the white cylinder between her long fingers. She gave me an expression of sympathy and asked if Sharon was asleep. I said yes, then I sat down on the hassock between Curt and Lou.

After a minute Lou tapped one of the papers. "Teddy Groner," he said. "You'll have to take him off your list of murder victims."

"I'd be interested to hear your reasons," said Curt.

"I was there, as you've noted. The day we went out in the boat Teddy said he wasn't feeling good and he sat on the bank. We didn't notice he'd started to swim out until he was half-way there. Ten feet from the boat he stopped swimming. He looked at me and I saw terror in his eyes. Then he slipped under the water. The others thought he'd just dived under the boat to come up on the other side, but I wasn't sure. A second later, when he didn't come up, I realized he'd had a cramp. I dived in. The water was murky and I could see only a dark shape drifting down. I tried to reach it, but my lungs gave out. I came up for air and yelled at the others and they started diving too. None of us saw him. It wasn't until they were dragging the cove for his body that I noticed the blood dripping off my fingers. I realized I'd been bleeding like hell all this time; I'd torn my arm on a nail getting on and off the boat while we were diving for him."

He held out his arm and showed Curt the scar on his forearm. I'd seen it before, a jagged crescent of shiny scar tissue. Curt leaned forward and examined the scar minutely, so long that Lou withdrew his arm, looking uncomfortable.

"Okay," said Curt. "Scratch Teddy. I don't need him anyway."

Lou read on, and after awhile said: "Here's another one—Jerry Blake."

Curt raised his brows. "You're sure it was an accident?"

Lou shook his head. "I'm almost sure it was suicide."

I was shocked. *"Jerry?* Why would he kill himself?"

"He was sick," said Lou. "Bad heart. He had... five, ten years if he took it easy. On the other hand he might go any minute. Only his wife and I knew. Jerry brooded a lot; he might have lived a moderate life if everything had been normal, but somehow the idea that he couldn't drink and couldn't hell around... well, Jerry just had to do it, that's all. Bought a cabin on the lake and took girls there. Got a helluva scare once when he had an attack there and the girl ran off and left him. Jerry told me about it; said he was afraid of kicking off while he was in the sack with some strange woman... embarrass his wife, raise hell with her future. Not long after that he went down to the store to do some late work; I was there, but I left early. You remember that night, Velda? I came home and said Jerry was acting strange. I was about to go back when I got the call that the store was on fire."

I nodded; remembering the night. I remembered early the next morning, when Lou had come in begrimed with smoke and said that Jerry was dead, and I should forget what he'd said about Jerry's strangeness.

"We were heavily insured," Lou went on, "and the insurance company tried like hell to prove it hadn't been an accident. They finally gave up. I found out later that the books were short by five thousand dollars... that's how Jerry had financed his high living. But if you mention it outside these walls I'll deny it. I don't think you'd be able to prove anything where the insurance company couldn't."

Curt looked tired. He stood up. "Don't bother to read any more."

Lou shrugged and handed the papers back to Curt. "Don't you have anything else?"

"Nothing," said Curt. "Let's go, Gaby."

Curt left with a strange, frozen expression on his face. I would have liked to talk to him, but there was no way I could see him alone; I felt tired and totally incapable of sleep. Somehow my irritation turned against Lou.

"You... smug citizen. Why didn't you give him the benefit of the doubt?"

Lou spread his hands. "What was I supposed to do? Say I was convinced when I wasn't?"

"You had your mind made up before."

"That isn't true." He squinted at me. "Did he hook you into helping him with that flimsy evidence?"

"He showed it to me—"

"But he has *nothing*, Velda. Couldn't you see that?"

I felt confused and angry. I started pacing the room, my fists clenched. "Why don't you just say I'm stupid. Tell me I haven't got the brains to deal with him?"

"Okay, you're stupid. You don't have the brains to deal with him."

"Ohhhhh." I threw up my hands and went into the bedroom. I lay down on the edge of the bed and lit a cigaret. After a minute Lou came in, calm and judicious, shaking his glass so the ice rattled.

"Velda, I understand this thing. Curt can't accept the guilt of his brother, so he's built up this fantastic theory in an attempt to deny it. He's smart in other ways, smart as hell, so naturally you assume he's right about this. But tell me, has he turned up one shred of concrete evidence? One single uncontradictory particle of proof?"

"Yes," I said, sitting up. "There was the note on his windshield—" I stopped abruptly. I didn't want Lou to know about our burglary of the Struble place. But Lou was nodding.

"He showed it to me. Curt said the handwriting was faked. Why couldn't *he* have faked it?"

"Oh Lou! And those phone calls in the middle of the night—"

"Couldn't he have made them?"

"But why?"

"Simple. Curt hates the county for what it did to his brother. He's trying to stir us up, get us to fighting each other." Lou chuckled, looking into his glass "Did I ever tell you about his experiment with the rats?"

I recalled that a couple of weeks ago Curt had wanted to trap some wild rats for an experiment. Lou had gotten the materials to build the cage and had helped him trap them in an old granary. But I didn't know what the experiment was about. "No," I said.

"He painted the tails of one group red and left the other group just as it was. Then he watched them exterminate each other—just like people."

I remembered Gaby's words: *"When he gets bored he kicks everything to pieces just to watch it fly apart."* I got out of bed and paced the room a couple of times. "Lou, your theory that he's doing this for revenge... it's just as fantastic as his—"

"You agree that his idea is fantastic?"

"It's fantastic that a killer has run loose for so many years."

"Too fantastic to be true."

"What about Sharon? Curt didn't attack her!"

"No," said Lou soberly. "That's something else again. I'll learn who did, and I'll take care of him myself. There's no need for official action."

I stopped and drummed my fingers on the bureau. My mind was fogged by the suddenness of events; I couldn't sort out my thoughts. Maybe a day or so on the lake, doing nothing but thinking...

Lou came up and put his hand on the nape of my neck. It was clammy cold from his glass. "Velda, you've let yourself get too deeply involved. Take Sharon and visit your mother for a few days. She can recover from her scare, and you from your... infatuation. .

I walked away and went into the living room, away from the voice of sweet reason. After awhile I lay down on the couch and closed my eyes; I'd decide tomorrow, I told myself, after I talked to Curt...

Next morning he came into the store with Gaby. It was rare for the two of them to appear together. Gaby's eyes were red and swollen and I thought she'd been crying.

"Hay fever," she said in a congested tone. "I cad hardly breed."

I looked at Curt. "I may visit my mother for a few days, get Sharon away."

He nodded absently. "It might be a good idea."

I felt as though I'd been told: *Thank you, your services are no longer required.* But I couldn't be sure until I talked to him alone. That evening I left Lou working in his shop and drove out to their place. We sat on the front porch—all three of us, and I told him about Lou's reaction. Curt was non-committal and vague; I felt like a third wheel. It was a hot night; mosquitoes whined in my ears and the leaves hung still as a painted backdrop. It was the kind of evening when the earth makes you feel like a stranger who doesn't belong. I felt a vague sadness, as on the last day of vacation, or at the end of a love affair. Around nine Gaby went inside to grill some cheese sandwiches. I had just turned to Curt when I felt it; a faint shimmering, a tightening of the air. A shock wave ruffled my hair, then a thunderous blast blew the doors open and shattered the windows. By the time I recovered my senses Curt was gone. Then I heard him inside the house shouting Gaby's name.

I ran into the kitchen. Curt was on the floor beside Gaby; her blouse hung in bloody shreds, and blood oozed from her face and neck. My nose filled with the stench of gas and the salty reek of blood. Curt looked up; I read the fear and guilt in his eyes and I thought, Gaby is dead, and Curt will never forgive himself. Then I saw his lips moving and I realized I'd been deafened by the explosion. I bent closer and shouted: "Is she alive?"

"Yes!" he shouted. "But losing blood. First aid kit in the bathroom. Then get your car up to the door."

I did as I was told. He tore up her skirt to make tourniquets for her arms and held his thumbs to the pressure points of her neck. As he carried her to the car, I saw the trail of blood she left on the wooden porch and I thought, She'll never make it.

I took the short cut to Connersville past Lake Pillybay. The third time I slid around a curve, Curt said in a calm voice from the back seat: "Don't rush. I've got the bleeding under control."

I slowed down and asked: "What happened?"

"Oven blew up. There was a fruit jar inside; slivers gashed her head and arms. She must have been bending over when it happened; the cuts all point downward."

"Curt, do you think—?"

"I think, yes. But I'll look into it later."

At the hospital they rushed her into the emergency room. A couple of minutes later an intern came out. "She needs whole blood. You know her type?"

"AB," said Curt. "Rh-negative."

The doctor winced. "That's rare. We may have to put out a radio call—"

I jumped up. "That's Lou's type. Rh-positive."

"Call him," said Curt.

I called Lou; he answered on the extension in his shop. He said he'd bring Sharon and come right over. He must have broken all speed records; I had no idea his pickup would go that fast. Within twenty minutes he was lying on a table next to Gaby. They had her bandaged so that not even her eyes showed. I could see an inch of her forehead above the gauze; it was a pale deadly yellow beneath her tan, but the doctor said her greatest danger was shock and loss of blood. He thought she'd live.

When we were back out in the waiting room, Lou said: "I think I know how it happened."

Curt turned from his pacing. "How?"

"I sell the same kind of stoves, you know. The oven has two walls, and the area between them is packed with insulation. If something should happen to the insulation—say mice ate it—gas would collect in the dead air space until it exploded."

It sounded reasonable to me, but Curt shook his bead violently. "Somebody knew she had hay fever. Somebody sneaked in and turned on the oven while we were talking out front. He knew she couldn't smell. He tried to kill her."

His tone was flat and metallic, like stones falling on a slate roof. He turned his back to us and looked out the window. Lou whispered to me: "You'd better go and visit your mother. He's liable to go over the edge."

I looked at Curt's stony face; I didn't believe he was in danger of going over. On the other hand, he didn't seem to need me. I looked at Sharon sprawled awkwardly asleep in a tubular aluminum chair. My folks lived only fifteen miles away, closer than Sherman. I decided to go.

My parents are the old-fashioned type; they greeted my wee-morning-hours arrival with open curiosity, but postponed their questions until breakfast. By this time they'd decided I'd quarreled with Lou. They disapproved—not of the quarrel, but of my departure. Groenfelder women have traditionally stayed on the home ground and fought it out toe-to-toe with their spouses. I didn't want to bring up Anne's death and I didn't want them to know what had happened to Sharon, so I let their misapprehension stand.

That afternoon I called the hospital, but they wouldn't let me talk to Gaby. The head nurse crooned that she was out of danger but receiving no calls. I asked for Curt, but they could give me no help and they gave me his number in Sherman. I called there and got no answer. I rang Lou and got the same negative result.

Another day was all I could take. I left Sharon there and told Mother I was going home to Sherman. Instead I went to Connersville. The receptionist at the hospital said I could see Gaby during visiting hours, in thirty minutes. I sat down to wait. The only other person in the room was a man whose face was three-fourths hidden by his newspaper. The visible one-fourth was enough for identification; I'd seen those sparse, carefully combed black hairs before.

"Boggus," I said. "Detective Boggus, what are you doing here?"

He put down his paper and moved to a chair beside mine. "Guarding the patient," he said. "Seeing that she gets no unwanted visitors."

"Somebody could sneak by in a hospital uniform."

He pursed his lips and smoothed his hair. "Well... I wanted to sit in the corridor but they wouldn't let me. I couldn't help that, could I?"

"You know where Curt is?"

"I'm not supposed to say." Unnecessarily, he added: "I don't know." After a moment he cleared his throat. "Incidentally, is he straight?"

"How do you mean?"

"I mean in the head. The lady upstairs got hurt when a stove blew up.

Okay, it could be attempted murder like he says, but a stove's a damned awkward weapon. I can't help remembering that the last killer he staked me out on turned out to be a fag and his boyfriend. That's why I ask if Friedland's straight."

I saw the receptionist beckoning. "He's straight," I said, getting up. "Don't sleep on the job."

The receptionist told me Room 220. I went up and found Gaby lying flat on her back, her neck and shoulders bandaged. She gave me a dreamy, drugged smile. "Velda... they say I won't be scarred."

"Good. Where's Curt?"

She frowned as though trying to place the name. "He was here... was that yesterday... ?"

I saw she was too dopey to talk sense. I took her hand and squeezed it. "I'll find him. Don't worry. Detective Boggus is downstairs."

"Boggus." She giggled. "Have no fear, Boggus is here." Suddenly her voice raised in alarm. "Velda, Curt went back to that terrible place. They'll kill him there. They hate him, all of them. . ."

I walked out into the corridor, silently cursing hospital officials for drugging patients just before visiting hours. Then I had a chilling thought: Maybe it hadn't been the hospital. I found the floor nurse in her lighted cave down the corridor. "The patient in two-twenty, did you give her a drug?"

The woman gave me an icy frown. "Who are you?"

"I'm her sister-in-law. It's very important."

She consulted a chart. "Yes, fifteen minutes ago she received codeine. It would make her somewhat... hazy. She was complaining about the stitches, you know. She had nearly fifty."

"Thank you." I decided I was worrying too much. As I left the hospital, Boggus lowered his paper and gave me a nod, which was supposed to be reassuring. It didn't help, because Gaby wasn't my big worry now.

A quarter mile from Curt's house I could see the place was dark. I parked the car at the entrance to a cornfield and hiked the rest of the way. I was surrounded by silence as I stepped onto the front porch; I waited a moment, then the cicadas resumed their hysterical trilling. I took off my shoes, tiptoed forward and put my ear to the front door. It gave silently. I pushed it open and called Curt's name softly. There was no answer. I walked up to the second floor; the bed rooms were empty. A ladder led up to the attic where Curt had fixed up a study. I climbed up and pushed open the trapdoor. Above me Curt's voice hissed from the darkness: "Keep down!"

I slid out onto the floor and lay flat. The darkness in the studio was stygian; Curt had done the walls in black. I lay for a moment letting my eyes acclimate, then I used my peripheral vision as Curt had taught me. Curt sat on the floor beside the window with a rifle across his knees. I thought of a spider sitting in the middle of his web, waiting for someone to come along and twitch it.

"I think I've got him," said Curt. "He's out there watching the house. Smart of you to come in without using your lights. Might have scared him off. How's Gaby?"

"She's fine..." Suddenly it all seemed like a play. There couldn't be a killer out there watching the house; this was Sherman in the year 1964, not the Dark Ages....

"How do you know he's out there?" I asked.

"Phone wires cut," said Curt. "Electricity off. He wants me to run for it. That's why he didn't try for you."

I had a prickly feeling that Curt was crazy. Wasn't that the way paranoiacs were, everything had to fit their fantasy? Maybe the light company had cut off his lights, maybe a phone wire had fallen down. Wouldn't that be just as logical? I felt an urge to humor Curt, to do nothing to shake his fantasy.

"Who is it?" I asked.

"We'll soon know." Curt lit a cigarette, wedged it into the front sight of his rifle, and passed the glowing end along the window. *Pwwinnng!* A bullet crashed through the window and tore into the shingle roof.

The shock was so great that for a moment I thought the slug had struck me in the stomach. Immediately all my doubts disappeared. There's nothing quite as convincing as solid lead. There was a killer out there; there was a murderer loose in Sherman. I realized how soldiers must feel when they're on the front line and the awareness hits them: My God, they're trying to kill *me!*

"What are you going to do?" I asked.

"Capture him. Get a confession."

I was about to ask if he'd quit suspecting Lou but he silenced me: "Shh. He's coming in."

I looked but I saw only darkness. "How do you know?"

"I feel him," said Curt in an intense whisper. "He's scared, uneasy, but he's excited too. He likes the idea of killing me.... He's choked up with desire, the kind you feel for a woman. He's coming on in a crouch... soon he'll hit the trip-wire. It's attached to a couple of flash units, the kind they use for photographing game. I think that's what scared Sharon's horse. I looked around the spot and found pieces of melted plastic. They use it to coat flashbulbs so they won't explode—there!"

A brilliant flash showed a stocky, bunched figure turning away as though about to run. Curt flicked a switch; a spotlight stabbed down. Curt's voice rang out into the night.

"Hold it or I'll shoot!"

The figure froze.

"Turn around!"

I held my breath as the killer turned. It was Johnny Drew.

"We caught a rabbit," said Curt. "The wolf is still loose."

INTERLUDE

The Killer's Game

Control is the key. My father killed himself when I was eight, but not before he taught me control through his own lack of it. Noise drove him into a rage; he must have had a brain tumor but nobody knew. He kicked apart my games and cursed me when I laughed. I devised secret games, and I learned how to laugh deep down inside. I drank poison after he died; they thought I didn't understand; they kept saying, Don't ever do that again, it'll kill you, don't you understand? I understood that they were afraid of death. I wasn't, because it seemed like something that had already happened to me. It made me stronger than them because they were afraid and I wasn't. That's when I hit upon the game. Later I figured out that your own death ends the game. You keep it going as long as you can. That's one of the rules.

The year after that Teddy Groner and I built a campfire near the haystack. I was fascinated by the way the orange tongues of flame could lick something and make it shrivel and die. I yelled, Feed it feed it, and started throwing hay on the fire. Teddy screamed and tore at my arms. I looked up and saw his five-year-old sister Lotte on top of the stack, but I couldn't stop. After awhile the yellow tongues licked her and she fell. I had to move back but Teddy stood frozen. Afterwards his face was blistered and his hair burned to a crinkly mass which flaked and fell off under your fingers. He remembered nothing. I told Teddy's folks I'd been off across the pasture when the fire started, and Teddy couldn't deny it. Teddy was never right after that, but you couldn't tell it for awhile. He hated me; sometimes he'd charge me blubbering and swinging his fists, but he never knew why. When we were twelve we built a house of grass and sticks and sat inside smoking cigaret butts. The little house caught fire; there was no danger but Teddy ran in terror. When the fire was out we went to Teddy's house to tell his mother but she said he was in bed sick. He was out of school for two months. After that he stuttered, played with trucks like he'd done when he was six years old. But I could never be sure that someday he wouldn't remember that fire. When we went swimming that day, we took Teddy with us. He was supposed to stay on the bank but you couldn't depend on Teddy. He started swimming out to the boat, then he dived down. I knew he planned to swim under the boat and come up on the other side. I slipped off the other side and caught him as he rose. He was out of air so he didn't struggle long....

One thing led to another. The little girl's death led to Teddy's, and then I was never sure of the other boys who'd been on the boat. There was Mart, that big red-necked peasant whose only hold on Velda was that he'd laid her first and she wasn't sure the other boys had what he had. I watched them together out on their farm, and I knew that's all she wanted from him—even though she'd told herself it was love and family and children. Those picnics she used to fix... she never ate a damn thing because she couldn't wait until lunch was over and they could get on with the real reason she'd come out there. Afterwards—Mart never saw this part but I did—she'd kneel down over the stream and wash herself, then straighten her clothes and go home looking demure as a bride. I was sure Mart had seen me the day he came running up the hill. That afternoon I went back with a hammer. The tractor made so much noise—he had an old John Deere—that he didn't know I was behind him until I climbed up on the drawbar. I cracked him behind the ear and he stumped down in the seat. I stopped the tractor, pulled him off and dragged him to the gully. Then I plowed four full rounds (you don't think about what can happen while you're vulnerable, you just try to cut the time as short as possible) in order to finish the section of land he'd marked off. Then I drove the tractor to the edge of the gully, cramped those little front wheels, and jumped. The tractor came down on top of him, the steering wheel crushed his chest. I wiped my fingerprints off the wheel, brushed my tracks out of the sand and left. On the way back to town I met Barney Proctor on his way to take Mart fishing. (Barney didn't really like to fish; he just wanted to get away from Ethel.) He found Mart's body and apparently forgot about meeting me. But it was Teddy Groner all over again; someday he'd remember and wonder what I was doing out there. I waited until he was fishing alone under the railroad bridge. I split his skull with an axe while he was baiting his hook (at twelve-forty-five, which gave me fifteen minutes before the one o'clock freight). I'd always wondered how it would sound; like a huge steel door crashing, like a mountain of tin cans falling down. The train took care of the evidence. Actually, that was the only real emotional kick in it; the rest was the sort of intellectual satisfaction you get when everything clicks into place, the knowledge that all seams are straight, no loose ends are left to snag you while you aren't watching....

Anne was different. She looked like Velda—except that Velda gave an impression of control. Her claws were sheathed, her lips covered the sharp white teeth. With Anne you noticed the teeth first, and you knew she was a meat-eater. She might have been different, but Frankie pulled her cork and her true nature burst through the Southern Baptist upbringing. I began to notice how often she was the object of a fight. While two brawny louts battered each other there sat this tender young morsel on the side-lines with her legs crossed protecting that little muff which was the object of the brawl and looking vaguely bored by the whole thing. While blood and gore splashed on the floor, she'd be casing the joint to see who was next. I was younger then; I didn't understand the game as well. I knew it well enough to see Anne's game, but I didn't have a clear picture of my own. Maybe Anne did... or maybe it was instinct that turned her eyes in my direction. I know that any man will have a weak moment sooner or later, and I knew if I put it off until I couldn't help myself, she'd be in con-trol. So I took her when I really didn't give a damn one way or the other: it was at the lake on the Fourth of July. Everybody was there; the coves were full of boats and skiers—though not as many as these days. I nosed my boat up to one of those floating beer joints they launch every holiday and called out to her: "Get in, we'll go for a ride." She shrugged and got in; five years had passed since Frankie left but she still hadn't found anything worth caring about. I nosed through a screen of cattails and into a seclud-ed cove; from the main channel it seemed to lead into a slough, but there was a clearing in the middle of it. I killed the engine, pulled the bottle out from under the seat, and gave it to her. Schenley's Black Label, a little warm from the sun, and she took it down a good inch on her first pull. I slid my arm around her and started to kiss her but she stiffened up: "You bring me here to kiss me?" "No." I said. "Then why did you bring me here? Go on. Say it." I said it and she laughed. "Most guys are afraid to say it. I guess I'll let you." She had on a two-piece swimsuit, I don't remember what color. She just peeled off the bottoms and slid forward in the seat. Then she looked at me and waited; the rest was up to me. At one point in the oper-ation another boat came nosing into the cove; I bent under the dash like I was repairing a loose wire, but Anne raised the bottle in a toast. The other boat circled and left (it was a tourist couple also looking for privacy) and they never suspected that Anne was sitting there with her bare bottom on the seat. Anne looked at me with a lopsided grin (she'd had three more slugs of warm whisky) and said, "Finish what you started—if you can." She had style, Anne did. She dangled her hand in the water the whole time. Afterward she rolled out of the boat and hung in the water, then reached in and got the bottom of her suit and pulled it on... all very casu-al and debonair, as though she were an experienced, high-class whore and not just a twenty-three-year-old rural honky-tonk queen. . .

She never came to me; I had to go to her. She knew what I was after (at the time I played the sex game to the fullest, believing it was the only game I had going) and she liked to make me crawl. I set up a meeting in Kansas City; she was to meet me in the room, but she picked up a belligerent drunk in the hotel bar and brought him with her. I was supposed to fight him and drench the place with blood, but I just took out my knife and said to him: "You're in over your head, buddy. Shove off." He crabwalked backwards out of the room. Anne was drunk and thick-lipped; I knew she hated me then because she clawed me and dared me to use the knife on her. She started yelling and throwing things and I knew she wanted the hotel people to come and she wanted it to be in the papers and spread all over the home town. She wanted the whole world to come crashing down on her head and mine too....

I gave her money and she shut up. After that it was a game to see how much money she could get from me. The money was only a way of keeping score, like holes in a cribbage board. Every time I saw her she'd present me with a bill. She told me she didn't give a damn for me or money; she'd give Frankie every cent she got, but he wouldn't take it. He took nothing from her and she offered everything. I began to hate the name Friedland. On that last night she sent me a note to meet her in Connersville with five thousand dollars. She didn't say or else, but I knew. When I met her, she said Frankie had to leave town before he got in bad law trouble. She wanted enough money for both of them to start up elsewhere. I gave her a check—it didn't matter because I knew the game had run out. I followed her when she left, knowing she'd meet Frankie. (There was no plan in my mind; I was just watching for an opportunity.) She stopped outside the club and sat in her car. I pulled around the other side of the club and parked four cars away with my lights off. Soon a boy came out headed for the outside john. I heard Anne tell him she wanted to see Frankie. When he went inside, Anne lit a cigaret; I jumped out of my car and ran up while she was still blinded by the flare of the match. I put my left hand over her mouth and nose and jammed her head back against the seat. The cigaret burned my palm but I didn't know it until later. I already had my jackknife open in my hand. I whispered, "Goodbye, Anne," and then jabbed the blade in below her left jawbone. I yanked it toward the right as hard as I could; her head jerked and flopped; there was a gush of blood and a whistle of air and a gurgling sound. I got the check from her purse and went to my car for the heavy jack-handle. Frankie came out and spoke her name, then leaned into the car. I clubbed him in the back of the head and watched him fall on top of her. I hit him again and drove away. I stopped at a river and washed off the blood and got rid of the knife. Then I stopped at a roadside restaurant and ate a thick steak and potatoes. It was only then that I noticed the burn on my hand. It wasn't shaking at all.

But after Bernice, something warned me: That's one too many young, pretty, loose married women. One of these days somebody will come along and add two and two. It turned out to be Friedland; that fact gave me a weird feeling of powers outside my comprehension. I felt as though the fates were pulling my strings and all I could do was babble and make the proper hand motions....

Sandy was a thing I had to do. She and Anne had traveled in the same crowd, and it was possible Anne had said something about me. I kept putting it off because Sandy didn't interest me, but when Friedland came back... well, in a sense he killed her. I picked her up as she started to walk home from the tavern with her baby. I gave her a drink and drove her around, watching her suck on the bottle. It was clear from the way she trusted me that she suspected nothing. But after I left her at the house—then George tore into town—I knew Friedland could make something of the fact that I'd driven her home. I went into the silent house, tied Sandy's hands and feet, and woke her up. I wanted to talk to her first, but she was disappointingly drunk. I just held my hand over her nose and mouth; she twisted and turned in the bed for only a couple of minutes. Air is such a precious thing, we die so quickly without it. The baby started whimpering then; I was afraid it would wake the others and there'd be three more to deal with. Some people aren't cold enough to be true humanitarians. I am; I smothered the baby too. Then I dropped the match on the floor behind the stove, watched it flare, then left. Some players would hang around and sweat it out: Are they really dead? Did I leave a clue? I threw it in the lap of the gods and left, and once again they took care of me.

But still, the act was pointless from the beginning. Curt Friedland pushed me into it, and I don't like to be pushed.... No, it's not a question of liking, but of uncertainty. I'd never before been up against a man who understood the game, and I wasn't sure of the rules. The one good thing about the new development was Velda. She occupied the ideal listening post in the community and Friedland needed her. I'm not sure how he worked her into his game; perhaps she worked herself. If she'd loved Mart she would not have been vulnerable to Curt but she didn't, otherwise she'd have gone the same way Anne did. The Groenfelder girls love only once, and when they lose their man, they die in essence. Velda didn't die; she was still looking. Men saw the searching look in her eyes and thought they were the object—Johnny Drew, Jerry Blake—but they weren't. Curt seemed to fill the bill. Maybe Velda was attracted by the coldness which enabled him to manipulate people, and by his reckless disregard of life which brought him nearer and nearer the big question mark. Given another environment, another historical setting, Friedland would have been a superb professional killer. (He'd administer death gently, like a blessing, as it should he done.) Maybe Velda was drawn by the smell of death. Whatever it was, she changed, matured, and now she glows with life purpose. Friedland was the catalyst Velda waited for, and I...

CHAPTER SEVEN

Velda's Game

I'd never seen a man questioned before, but I know if I'd had anything to hide, I'd have told Curt before the night was over. He was a cold unfeeling machine; to him Johnny Drew was a locked box which had to be pried open. He tied Johnny to a chair in his black-walled studio and questioned him until I thought I would scream at the repeated questions, each one asked in a hundred different ways. Each time Johnny failed to answer, Curt slapped his doughy checks. I could see the object wasn't to hurt him physically, but to wear him down by repetition, the way the Chinese do with drops of water.

"Where've you been hiding?" Slap. "Did you kill Anne?" Slap. "Who're you working for? You've got four hundred dollars in your wallet. Who gave it to you? You're carrying a Husqvarna .270 rifle. Where'd you buy it? How'd you get these scratches on your hands? Who told you to kill me? How'd you make those phone calls? What's a phone jack? What's a bug? A transistor? Are you right-handed? You don't have insulated clippers. Who cut my electric wires for you?"

Johnny started out trying to sneer, but after an hour his face was a gory mask. His lips were cut on the inside and blood was drooling from his mouth.

"Maybe he isn't working for anybody," I said finally. "Maybe it's his own idea."

"Johnny doesn't have ideas. He's a boob. Aren't you a boob, Johnny?" Curt slapped Johnny's head back against the chair. "You don't know electronics, you don't know how a stove works, you don't know a goddam thing. The other guy set it up; you were just the voice on the line, the muscle, while the other guy walked around the community and showed his smiling face at the right time. Wasn't that it, Johnny?"

"Water..." said Johnny. "Give me a drink."

"That's encouraging. First words you've said. Velda, go down and get a glass of water."

I followed my flashlight beam down through the dark house to the kitchen. The furniture still lay on its side and dark stains remained where Gaby's blood had leaked. I got the water and hurried back upstairs. Curt took the glass, turned his back a moment, then held the glass to Johnny's lips. Johnny took a swallow, then coughed and spat.

"Salt water. You bastard!"

"You get fresh water when you talk. Ready?"

Johnny wasn't ready. Curt stood him up against the wall and got out his bow and arrows. They were barbed hunting arrows, not the round target points we'd been using. He fired three arrows around Johnny, one of them so close that it pinned his shirt to the wall. Greasy sweat rolled down Johnny's face, but he remained silent.

Curt handed the bow to me. "Take a couple of shots, Velda."

"I can't shoot, Curt. You know that."

"That's Johnny's worry."

My knees shook as I got up and fitted an arrow into the bow. Johnny faced me with his mouth open, his eyes wide. "Velda, you wouldn't—"

I don't know whether I would have or not. Curt may have wanted me to bluff, but I was pulling back on the bowstring and my fingers were sweaty... I lost my grip; the string twanged and an arrow quivered in the wall a foot from Johnny's ear.

"Good shot, Velda. Take another."

"Curt, I didn't aim—"

"Aim this time. For his belly. Even if he's punctured, he'll live long enough to talk—"

"No!" Johnny's face was gray behind the blood. "I made those phone calls. I hid out in Connersville."

"How'd you get your instructions?"

"A bartender gave me an envelope with money and instructions."

"Who gave them to him?"

"A kid delivered it. That's all I know. . ."

"Not enough, Johnny."

Curt walked to the wall and slammed Johnny down in a chair. I could-n't tell what he was doing; his body blocked my view. I saw Johnny's head forced back and I heard him gag. After a moment Curt stepped back and set a pill bottle on his desk.

"Those pills are to speed up your heartbeat, Johnny. It'll pound faster and faster until it bursts. It'll fill your insides with blood until you can't breathe. You'll choke to death on your own blood."

Veins stood out on Johnny's head. His face twitched. I picked up the pill bottle and saw that it contained Dexedrine tablets. They'd speed up Johnny's heartbeat, but they weren't fatal.

"Feel the heart pounding, Johnny? It takes fifteen minutes. Feel the blood racing? You can still talk...."

Johnny licked his brown-crusted lips. "If... if I talk, what?"

"I'll give you pills to counteract these. They'll carry you into dreamland."

"Okay... I... got instructions to kill you. He said you'd be here, the lights off and so on. I got four hundred in advance and would get another thousand when the job was done."

"How'd you get the instructions?"

"By... telephone."

"You didn't get the money by telephone."

"They... it was given to the bartender in an envelope."

Curt jumped to his feet. "What was the name of the bar?" He gave Johnny only a second to answer, then asked: "What did the bartender look like? Blond or brunet or bald? What time did you pick up the money? You can't answer, can you? I'm tired of screwing with you. *Tired*, you hear? You slimy goddam snake!"

His open hand caught Johnny's jaw and dumped him from his chair. I thought Curt had lost his temper, but then I saw it was only a pose. Curt helped Johnny back into his chair and spoke in gentle, friendly tones. "You've never heard of the Italian rat torture, have you, Johnny? They put a pair of hungry rats in a cage which fits around a man's neck. First the rats eat away the ears, then the nose, then the eyelids. Then they go for those bright shiny eyes. You can't look away, Johnny. You can't close your eyes. You have to stare at those sharp yellow teeth biting into your eyes the way you'd bite into a peach. I just happen to have a pair of hungry rats...."

He went to the corner and folded back a piece of heavy canvas. Beneath it was a metal bird cage containing two lean gray rats. They cluttered excitedly as Curt carried them toward Johnny. My stomach turned over. Curt held the cage against Johnny's cheek; the smell of blood excited them; they squealed and leaped against the side of the cage, their yellow teeth slashing. Johnny groaned and slumped in his chair.

Curt shook him; he lolled, a dead weight. Curt put the rats back beneath the tarpaulin, then threw the glass of salt water in his face. Johnny didn't move. Curt sat down and lit a cigaret.

"What are you going to do?" I asked.

"Wait until he wakes up." He glanced at his watch, then peered at me. I felt as though I'd been dragged over plowed ground against the furrow; I must have looked that way because Curt said: "It's three a.m. There are beds downstairs. You can lie down and rest. I'll wake you if I need you."

I climbed down the ladder and went into the bedroom. I lay down on Curt's bed, amid the smell of his tobacco and after-shave lotion. I didn't intend to sleep, but I did. Dawn glowed warm in the windows when I awoke. The house was draped in silence. I climbed up to Curt's studio, pushed open the trapdoor, and shoved my head through. The gruesome scene struck me all at once, like a hammerblow between the eyes. I gave a little shriek and let the trapdoor fall. I clung to the ladder breathing hard. Could I have imagined the sight? Fatigue, loss of sleep, could that have made me see Johnny Drew lying on the floor with the feathered shaft of an arrow protruding from his chest? Numbly I pushed open the trapdoor; it was real, Johnny Drew was cold meat, as lifeless as a roll of canvas. Although I'd never seen a corpse outside a coffin, I knew there was no point in checking Johnny's pulse.

I lowered the trapdoor and ran downstairs; there was no sign of Curt on the first floor. I ran out the front door and tried to stop, but my momentum was too great. I ran into the arms of Sheriff Wade, who said, "Velda, what the hell—?" I stared into Lou's wide, dumbfounded eyes and I felt my head swimming, the earth tilting. The light faded, and I thought, How corny and feminine, to faint at a time like this....

I awoke in my own bed, and there was young Doctor Nash, with a thin moustache and a greasy bedside manner he must have learned from TV. He was dismantling a hypodermic needle and putting it into a tray. He smiled at me—a process which divided his moustache into separate hairs—and said: "Just lie back, Mrs. Bayrd. I've given you a sedative which should let you rest all day."

"Doctor, you didn't..."

My head whirled suddenly. When it cleared the doctor was outside the room talking in hospital tones to my husband. I wanted to get out of bed but I was caught in a pool of lassitude as heavy as sweet molasses. My lids drooped shut and I was looking into a well spiraling down and down. A light glowed at the bottom like a tiny coin; somebody's face smiled up at me. *Just drift down,* said a voice in my head, *drift down.* I drifted down: I wore a filmy garment which drifted around me like cobwebs. It was Curt waiting down there for me; his hands stripped the lace from my body and he laughed: "Can't you ever say what you want, Velda? Won't you ever be honest with yourself?" I was naked, and his hands passed over my body leaving trails of fire. Horrified, I watched Curt unzip his trousers; he came toward me and I saw that he held a huge hypodermic needle in his hand. I put my hands down to protect myself, saying: "No, I don't want to sleep; I want to know what's happening..." Suddenly there was Gaby dressed in a nurse's uniform. She seized my hands and pulled them away, saying: "Don't be childish. Isn't this what you wanted?" Curt laughed and jabbed, and I felt it go all the way in, up through my stomach and into my lungs until I couldn't breathe....

I opened my eyes; my covers were damp with sweat. A low sun cast a red glow on the opposite wall. *Day is done.* Outside I heard the mewling of dogs. I got out of bed, staggered to the window, and looked out. A panel truck had parked in the drive. Through the wire mesh I saw the mournful lace of a bloodhound. I slipped on my housecoat and walked into the front room to look out the other window. In the front yard stood Sheriff Wade, his deputy and Lou. The sheriff was dressed as usual, but Deputy Hoff was armed for a siege. Two pearlhandled forty-fives hung low on his hips, tied

down with leather thongs. Slung on his back was a rifle. I half-expected to
see grenades hanging from his belt. Hoff was walking around in small circles, hitching up his belt and spitting on the ground. The sheriff was talking to Lou. Silently I raised the window and listened:

"...like to have you with us Lou, since you're a good hand with guns. He's
somewhere over there in Brush Creek. The hounds will find him. But the
more men we have, the less chance of anybody getting hurt."

"How about Friedland? You plan to take him alive?"

"He'll get his chance. If he doesn't take it " The sheriff shrugged. "It'll be
a better chance than he gave Johnny Drew. Torturing a man in my county..." For a moment the sheriff seemed choked by indigestion, then he said:
"How about it? You want me to deputize you?"

Lou shook his head. "First place, I don't know Brush Creek. I wouldn't be
much help. In the second place, I don't like hunting a man with dogs, no
matter what he might have done."

The sheriff nodded curtly. "Okay, Lou. Whatever you say. Let's go, Bobby."

They jumped in the panel truck and roared off. Watching Lou walk back
to the house, I felt proud of him for not joining the hunt. I ran into my
room and crawled back in bed just as Lou pushed the door open. "Velda?"
I fluttered my eyelids and he came in. "Velda, they're hunting Curt. They
wanted to question you but I said that you were asleep." He sat down on
the edge of the bed. "I want you to tell me why you were at Curt's house
this morning."

"How did you know I was there?"

"Your mother called and asked if you'd arrived home safely. That's when
I started looking for you."

I swore at myself for forgetting. Mother always called to see if I'd gotten
home all right; she'd been doing it ever since Anne's death.

"But... why'd you bring the sheriff?"

"He just happened to be with me. He had a search warrant for the house;
he suspected Curt of burglarizing his office. Now I've answered your questions. You answer mine."

I told Lou that Gaby had given me a message for Curt. I went on to tell
him what had happened at Curt's house after I got there. I told him
because I wanted a favor from him; I wanted him to join the posse and
keep them from killing Curt. Lou hesitated; the deputy might be gun-
happy, but he couldn't shoot. If he got close enough to hit Curt, he'd be
close enough to take Curt alive. "If he wanted to," I said, then I told him
about the fight the two had when Curt first arrived. Lou agreed to go, provided I took the sleeping capsule the doctor had left for me.

"I'm still half-asleep, Lou. But leave it there, and I'll take it."

"No, Velda," he said in a tone you'd use on a feeble-minded patient. "I
don't want you tearing through the hills." He held the capsule out

between his fingers. "Open your mouth."

I opened my mouth and let him put the capsule on my tongue. I felt like a little baby robin. I giggled and realized I was still giddy from the shot that morning. But I had enough sense to work the capsule in between my cheek and my gums, so that when I swallowed the water Lou handed me, the capsule stayed in my mouth. He left the room, and I spat out the capsule. I went to the window and watched Lou raise the hood of my car and jerk something loose, then climb in his pickup and drive off.

I ran out and raised the hood. I stared at the mass of wiring for several minutes without finding anything loose. I got out the repair manual, opened it to a photo of the engine, and compared the two. There was something visually awry in the area around my distributor. I tugged gently on all the wires until I found the loose one; it was the connection to the coil. I connected it and tried the car; it started. I drove toward Lake Pillybay. I wasn't sure where Curt would go, our last few meetings had been in the open, but he'd once pointed to a narrow cleft in a rock and said there was a cave inside. Frankie had found it once and showed it to Curt; as far as he knew nobody else was aware of it. I pulled the car off the road a quarter mile from the cave and piled branches over it. The distant yap of dogs sent shivers up my spine. I started walking, congratulating myself on my cleverness at outwitting Lou with the capsule and the car. Gradually I became aware of a coldness on my body. Only then did I realize I'd come out naked except for my thin nightgown. It was strange to trudge through the woods without underclothing; occasionally the wind whipped up my gown and gave me a chilling, intimate caress.

But I found the place. A sheer cliff rose up beside a narrow ravine full of dead leaves and humus. No trees grew right in the ravine, which left a ten-foot-wide open space between the woods and the cliff. I stopped at the edge of the clearing and called softly: "Curt."

There was no answer. I called again.

A strong hand gripped my arm. Curt's voice whispered: "Velda, here you are again, wearing white at night."

"I couldn't think of everything. I came to warn you—"

"Shhh. Go inside and wait. I'll see if you were followed."

I squeezed through the cleft and groped my way inside. I smelled dust, decay, bat manure and gas. As my eyes got used to the dark, I saw that the smell of gas came from a tiny butane stove. By the pale blue flame I saw the two suitcases which held Curt's recording apparatus. A coil of wiring lay on the cavern floor, plus a tool kit, a lumped sleeping bag and a case of groceries. I heard Curt come behind me and I asked:

"How'd you move this stuff in so quick?"

"I put it here weeks ago... all but the recording stuff. It was a second line of defense."

I said: "You predict everything, don't you?"

He laughed without humor. "Not quite. Gaby's accident for one thing. Johnny Drew's death for another—"

"You didn't kill him?"

He sighed. "Velda, I've told you. I didn't come here to kill anybody."

"Well, I thought, maybe by accident—"

"By accident Johnny happened to pass in front of the window. Somebody outside was waiting for that moment. It was a good shot. I found Gaby's bow in the brush a hundred yards away. I lost the killer's trail when he waded a stream. I tried to pick it up again, but it was still too dark. When I got back, your husband was there, with the sheriff. What did they do to you?"

I told him about the hunt and the gun-happy Hoff. Curt lit a candle and I saw that his hair was wild, his eyes puffy, his checks stubbled. He didn't look as though he'd slept since the night Gaby was injured.

"You know who it is?" I asked.

"Johnny Drew died without talking," he said.

"What do you plan to do now?"

"Stay here until the hunters decide I've left the county."

"I'll stay with you."

"No you won't."

"You plan to tie me up and carry me home?"

He looked at me for a moment, then he handed me a rifle. "Put on something dark and keep watch at the entrance. I'll catch a nap."

I threw a blanket over my shoulders and wedged myself in the mouth of the cavern. I could hear the chilling yelp of the hounds. Once I heard a distant gunshot; I decided something had spooked Deputy Hoff. I pictured Curt trying to give himself up to those men, and I knew he'd die the moment they saw him.

The time dragged slowly. The coldness of the rock seeped through the blanket and numbed my back and buttocks. Breezes found their way up my legs like cold searching fingers. The hour reached midnight, one o'clock. I no longer heard the hounds; I decided the search had been recessed for the night, all the hunters gone home to bed. I felt totally alone, like the last woman on earth. The moon slid in and out of the clouds, creating weird shadows which humped through the forest. The wind whispered and moaned through the leaves. There was nothing human out there; nothing to give me comfort. I went back inside and lay down beside Curt. He slept silently, without snoring. He smelled of clothing worn too long, but I didn't mind. I tickled him with my hair and he snorted, wiping his nose on the back of his hand. He shifted to a new position and put his arm around me. "Gaby " he mumbled. I put my hand under his shirt and rubbed the warm muscular back. He slid his hand down, found the hem of the nightdress and tugged upward. I lifted myself up to help, then relaxed against him. He ran his hands down the curve of my back and touched my buttocks. I suppose that's what made him aware because there was a considerable difference in size. He stiffened slightly but didn't withdraw his arms. "Velda?" He wasn't questioning my identify, but something else. "Are you awake?"

"Yes," I said. "Wide-awake."

I could count on my fingers the times I've enjoyed it... I mean when the flood of emotion picks me up and swirls me to a place of no-thought, no-time, no-existence. With Mart a couple of times, with Lou perhaps once, and there in the cave with Curt. I tried to tell him without sounding grateful or obsequious, but he merely chuckled. "I remember the best food I ever had, it was cold and windy and I'd been driving cattle for half a day. I stopped and had a cold ham sandwich with ketchup and I've never tasted anything as delicious since."

"If you're saying I was sex-starved..."

"I was thinking of the excitement—"

"You rationalize everything until it's meaningless." I stood up and pulled down my nightdress. I thought of the shower I usually took after sex, but I didn't feel dirty. Those sanitary operations belonged to another woman, a certain Mrs. Bayrd. I wanted nothing more to do with her.

"Speaking of food," I said.

"I'll get it."

"Your job is to guard the cave. Go, great hunter."

He went. I warmed a can of Vienna sausage and fried eggs on the little stove. Curt came back and squatted beside the fire and ate from a paper plate. After a minute he said: "It's about daylight. You think you can get out and contact Gaby?"

My heart sank. I didn't want to leave the cave; there were too many problems outside. "You just want to get rid of me."

He shook his head. "Somebody's got to tell her to put plan 'C' into effect. She'll know what to do."

Jealousy is a childish emotion, but there it was. "Why don't you tell me?"

"It's complicated. First of all it means I've got the local law on my back. I've established a certain contact with the state police; he doesn't know you but he knows Gaby. I'm not sure he'd act on your word. Tell Gaby plan 'C,' that's all you have to do."

I said I'd try. Curt took a wrinkled plaid shirt and cotton trousers from his sleeping bag and said I could wear them. I pulled off my nightdress, feeling neither shy nor bold to be standing nude before him; just very natural. I let him slide the shirt onto my arms. The cold morning air drew my nipples tight; Curt's touch sent the pulse surging through my veins. I turned in his arms and drew his head down in a kiss; I felt an urge to let my legs go limp and pull him down to the floor with me. I was a glutton, I knew; when Gaby came back there would he no more chances, and I wanted to store up memories for the future. But I sensed Curt's urgency, and withdrew my embrace. While he was rolling up my trouser legs he said:

"Don't go home, you understand? Don't talk to anybody. Just call Gaby and then hide out."

I left, feeling a deep serenity beneath the overlay of urgency. I felt like a college girl sneaking home after a night in her boyfriend's dormitory. I reached the car and drove out, planning to sneak into Sherman and call from the store. Just outside Sherman I rounded a curve and nearly crashed into a pair of livestock loading chutes which had been placed across the road. I slammed on the brakes and skidded to a halt; I looked out the window and saw Joe Riley, former pool-hall bum of Sherman, approaching the car with a deer rifle. A deputy sheriff's badge gleamed on his dirty denim shirt.

"Misses Bayrd. They lookin for you all over creation. Don't move. I'm a legal deputy, 'powered to shoot."

I could only sit cursing my lack of caution while he ran around the car and got in on the other side. "Now jest ease around on the shoulder and out the other side. I reckon I better take you home."

As I drove, Joe never took his eyes off me. Now and then his gaze wandered down to my bosom, and I suspected that Curt's oversized shirt had gaped open to reveal a breast or two. It occurred to me that I might seduce Joe and escape. I noticed his yellowed teeth and realized I couldn't do it without throwing up. Still I tried stopping the car and pretending an urgent call of nature, but Joe smirked and said: "I reckon you can hold it for another mile, Missus Bayrd." So like a sacrificial lamb I drove up our drive and there was Lou and Sheriff Wade waiting in front of the house. There was no sign of Deputy Hoff. The sheriff lumbered over to the car looking angry enough to chew off the barrel of his .38. He yanked open the door and seized me by the arm. "I'm through playin games with you, little lady. Where'd you leave that murderin' sonuvabitch?"

"Sheriff, please—" His hand was a vise biting through my biceps. Lou walked up.

"Hold it, Sheriff. Maybe she doesn't know about Bobby."

"Come on."

The sheriff pulled me out of the car and I had to run to keep from falling. He threw open the back of the panel truck. Deputy Hoff lay inside. He'd swagger no more; an arrow had gone all the way through his neck, just below the ears. In his khaki gabardines, he resembled a deer being carried home to he butchered. I gasped.

"But Curt couldn't have—" I caught myself. "I don't know anything about this, Sheriff. I'm... sorry. About your nephew."

"Nothing gonna bring him back to life." The sheriff was a man stunned by grief, half out of his mind. His voice was gruff. "Thing I gotta do is get the guy who did it. Now you tell where he is and maybe I won't put you under arrest—"

"I don't know *anything*."

"All right, Velda." He reached for the handcuffs on his belt, but Lou said:

"Give me a minute, Sheriff." Lou took my arm and marched me in the house, into the bedroom. He closed the door and seized my shoulders. "Now listen. Don't you understand that Curt's a wanted man? You can't protect him. He killed an officer—"

"He didn't."

"Were you with him last night? Is that how you're sure?"

I kept my mouth closed.

"Velda, you're wearing the proof. Those clothes..."

"Yes, I was with him."

Lou nodded. "All right. Tell me where he is."

"But Lou... they'll kill him on sight. You know that."

"Just tell me. He can give himself up to me. Look." He reached in his shirt pocket and held a badge out in his palm. "I'm a special deputy. I'll bring him in and see that he gets a fair trial."

My eyes caught that crescent scar on his forearm. I remembered Curt staring at it that night; I recalled how emphatically he'd warned me against coming home. I realized the scar couldn't have been made by a nail...

"Velda," Lou was saying. "I don't want to turn you over to the sheriff. I'm trying to help you. For God's sake, think of Sharon, think of your family. You don't want to go to jail as Curt's accomplice. He's ruined himself, but you don't have to follow his example. Just tell me where he is..."

A picture came into my mind; Teddy Groner in the high school group photo, smiling. He had even white teeth, with canines noticeably prominent, extending a quarter of an inch down past his incisors. Looking at Lou's scar I could almost see Teddy's teeth sinking into Lou's arm in a desperate underwater struggle. I thought of other things... Lou practicing with the bow until he could shoot almost as good as Curt... Lou calling me at three a.m. on the night of Anne's murder, telling me the clerk had forgotten to relay my call. I remembered all the electronic equipment in Lou's shop, and the way he always seemed to know what went on in the store even when he wasn't there. I remembered Johnny Drew confessing that he'd made the calls, and realized that Lou's presence in bed did not absolve him of guilt. I thought of Sharon being attacked by her own father and my mind recoiled in horror. I forced myself to say...

"He's in the old Boy Scout cabin, Lou. But I want to go with you."

Lou shook his head. "You're weak, Velda. Your mind isn't working too well. You stay here and rest." He got busy at the little tray beside my bed. "Those pills aren't strong enough. The doctor left something else . . ."

I watched him fill the hypodermic needle and I thought of air bubbles injected into the vein, which kill you so quickly and leave no evidence...

I ran. He was so engrossed in his task that I made it out of the house. The sheriff pulled his gun but hesitated: I guess he'd never shot a woman before. Joe stared at me without raising his gun; I think he forgot he had one. I jumped in the car and drove down the lane, my tires squealing. West of town I skidded around the roadblock and drove on toward the lake. I didn't want to lead them too close to the cave. I drove the car into a cornfield and tried to wipe out the tracks. Then I walked a mile into the woods, crawled into a hazel-brush thicket, and waited. When darkness came, I went on to the cave. I called Curt's name and went in. Curt was behind me.

"Did you reach Gaby?" he asked.

I started to explain, but a brilliant light flashed behind me. Lou's voice said: "Put your hands up, both of you."

I whirled, but saw only a disc of blinding white light. Lou laughed. "I've been with you all day, Velda. You underestimated me, just like you've been doing all your life." His voice hardened. "Turn around and put your hands against the wall. I carry a sawed-off shotgun. I could get you both with one shot."

I turned slowly, and Curt whispered without moving his lips. "Talk. Get him talking."

I made two tries before my voice worked. "You...I can't believe you'd attack Sharon, Lou. You must have had Johnny do that?"

Lou laughed. It wasn't a pleasant sound. If I'd heard it in a crowded restaurant I'd have turned to stare in horror at the man who'd made it. I realized what Lou had kept bottled up all these years; he'd stepped out of the human race a long time ago....

"You didn't think it out, Velda. That little scare wasn't nearly as bad as having her learn I was a mass murderer. Think of her carrying that burden. Your lover was making you look too closely at me, and I couldn't handle you both at once. I had to find some way of turning off your suspicion."

"I don't understand how you used Johnny Drew."

"I caught him stealing from the hardware store. I had him then, but he couldn't kill; he botched the attempt to kill you, Curt, even though he hated you enough."

"Why did you kill the deputy?" I asked.

"To get the sheriff mad enough to shoot Curt on sight. I was intrigued by the idea of having the law do the job for me, but—" He stopped abruptly. "I see your idea; keep me talking until the sheriff arrives, is that it? Sorry to disappoint you, the sheriff went in the other direction, he's five miles away by now. But I don't mind talking. Excuse me while I sit down." There was a pause, then: "All right, move just a little closer together, your shoulders touching, that's fine. You make a handsome couple, you know. I originally had the thought of catching you two in bed together and killing you both. I could have gotten away with it; pillar of the community loses head in fit of jealous rage. But you somehow kept clear of the sex scene—that is, until recently. I sense a new attitude in you, Velda. You've had yourself a nice little tumble and you're happy, aren't you? Happy enough to die?"

My heart stopped, because I knew he meant it. Curt asked:

"How would you explain it?"

"Oh... that you used my wife as a shield. Or perhaps you killed her and then I killed you. Either way I'll be a hero. I never plan in advance...."

Lou kept talking, and Curt drew him out. I listened in horrified fascination while he told about watching Mart and me, about killing Anne and Barney and another girl whom we'd thought had merely run away from home. He'd buried her in the dam of a pond he was building. And Jerry Blake had been simple: Lou's hardware store and the drugstore shared the same storehouse. Jerry was heavily addicted to morphine toward the end; he took to stealing it from the storeroom, shooting himself when he went to the store at night. Lou waited until he'd given himself a shot, then opened a butane tank, hooked up a timed electric spark gadget, and was home before the explosion occurred. Why? His voice was diffident. Lou had concealed Johnny's theft, but Jerry had discovered the shortage and blamed Lou. Gaby's stove... it had happened the way he'd explained, except that Lou was the one who'd taken out the packing.

"Remember how Gaby complained that her oven wouldn't hold heat?" he asked. "The gas built up in there for two weeks before it blew up. It could've happened any time. It had nothing to do with her hay fever."

"Did you plan to kill her?" asked Curt.

"Oh no," said Lou. "Not at that time, anyway. I wanted you to take her out of the game; it was too much trouble to watch both of you and Velda too. Then a couple of days ago, when both Velda and Gaby were gone, and I thought we could have our private little game—"

"But you threw in Johnny Drew."

"A pawn," said Lou. "I was testing your defenses. I didn't know you had Velda."

They were like two friends rehashing a card game. I had to pinch myself mentally to realize that death lay at the bottom of it.

"We could still have the game," said Curt. "Let Velda go."

Lou gave a short laugh. "Impossible. She knows too much, Gaby too...."

"Gaby knows nothing."

"Suspects. That's enough...."

"You have to keep killing, don't you? Once you start it's the answer to every dilemma. How many of those others were murder?"

"Oh, you were right on several. Teddy Groner, as you suspected, bit me underwater. I made up that story of the nail on the spot, then I was stuck with it. I figured it would trip me up someday. The woman who supposedly hanged herself... I made the mistake of thinking she was willing when she wasn't. The man who was eaten by hogs, the one who killed himself with the shotgun, they were theories I wanted to work out... though I told myself I wanted to buy their land cheap—"

"You know how it ends, Lou?" said Curt in a mild tone of curiosity. "You'll meet somebody else with the game and it'll be your turn. That's the only way it can end, with your death. You're committing suicide the hard way."

"Of course," said Lou. "I figured that out myself. But you'll never—"

Suddenly everything dissolved in a thunderous explosion. A terrific weight slammed against my back and threw me against the face of the cliff. Darkness closed in. I was sure Lou had fired and I thought, Heaven is a rocky place. Then I realized I was lying on the cave floor. I felt sticky warmth trickle down my face and knew it was blood running from a bump on my forehead. Hands caught my armpits and hoisted me to my feet; I turned and looked into Curt's face. I was silly from shock; I laughed at the white limestone dust which coated his face, hair and eyebrows. His moist lips looked brilliant red. He looked like a character in a Japanese play. I heard my own laughter echo inside my head, and I realized I was deaf. Suddenly weak, I fell against him and clung for support.

Not until then did I remember Lou. I looked at where he'd been and saw only a slab of limestone.

"Lou—?" I had to shout in his ear. "What happened?"

Curt got the flashlight and shone it on the cave floor. The first thing I saw was the shotgun. Then Lou's hand, clutching the stock. I followed the hand to an arm, and the arm to the vast slab of limestone as big as a grand piano. I saw Lou's head, and I turned away quickly and hid my face. But the image remained; his face was swollen, his eyes bulged like those of a rat caught in a trap. I felt no grief, he had ceased to be my husband and became a monster. For an instant I sensed a whole race of such creatures living among humans, saying the right things and performing the correct actions and all the while playing their little death games. How many women, I wondered, will go to bed tonight with a monster?

Curt took my hand and led me toward the rear of the cave. "There's a rear exit," he was saying. "I sabotaged the entrance in case they trapped me, put a charge of dynamite behind a loose slab. It happened that Lou was sitting right under it."

"How'd you set it off?"

Curt showed me the hidden wire running into his shoes. There was a battery pack strapped inside his trousers. He took a reel of tape from his recording apparatus and explained that he'd started the machine as we entered the cave. He'd known I was being followed, but figured the killer would talk only if he thought he had the upper hand.

"Did you know it was Lou?"

"I... was almost sure when I saw the stuffed mice."

"So *long*? And you didn't tell me?"

"You had all the information I had, Velda. But you wouldn't believe it. Come on, let's find a new hiding place. That explosion will draw attention."

We crawled out of a hole just large enough to squeeze through. As I emerged into the night, a flashlight blinded me. I started to retreat, but Gaby's voice said:

"Velda, Curt. It's me."

She was standing beside a state trooper, looking almost as pale its her bandages. I didn't watch as she and Curt embraced. The trooper was a heavy-necked clean-featured six-footer, the kind of depersonalized All-American boy you find in state police uniforms. He came over to me and bandaged my forehead. "I'm Trooper Carson, and you're..."

"Velda Bayrd," I said in a tone which was neither sad nor exultant. "My husband is dead inside. He's a murderer. Curt has his confession."

A helicopter waited at the top of the ridge. As we flew out, Gaby explained that she'd tried to phone Curt and had gotten strange responses from the operator; immediately she'd put plan "C" into effect. She'd known about the cave and had been able to lead the troopers in. They set us down on the airfield outside Connersville. I started toward the taxi stand and Curt called after me:

"Where are you going?"

I turned and saw him and Gaby standing together. There was no place for me between them. I felt bitterness rise inside me. "Do you care?" I gave him no time to answer. "No, you don't. You were playing the same game Lou was. It wasn't as deadly as his; it might be more human if it were. With you there's no emotion. No involvement. You treat us as though you were some being from the stars. You're cold and cruel and heartless—"

Suddenly I ran out of steam. "No, I'm sorry. You did it to get Frankie out of jail."

Gaby came forward and took my hand. "Come with us. We'll get Frankie out and then go to the islands."

I could see that she understood my problem. I wondered how many times she'd watched women fall in love with her husband. I felt my stubbornness come in and give me strength: "You might persuade me," I said. "But I've got a daughter. What can I say when she learns her father was a monster? What will I tell her?"

"To... be strong," said Gaby.

"But I feel that I did it to her. I married him. I..."

I looked past Gaby and saw Curt, his achingly handsome face frozen, and that vague superior amusement in his eyes. Comprehension flooded in like a sunrise. Many people had fallen victim to my husband, but *he* was Curt's victim. My husband had toyed with them, but Curt had toyed with Lou, like a cat with a mouse. I realized that Curt would go on, having discovered the game behind the game, to seek other men like Lou. And next time there'd be no brother to free, just the sheer thrill of... hunting the hunter.

I turned and walked away. Nobody called me back. I didn't really expect it. *Be strong, Gaby*, I said to myself.

THE END

DAN J. MARLOWE BIBLIOGRAPHY

Doorway to Death (1959)*
Killer With a Key (1959)*
Doom Service (1960)*
The Fatal Frails (1960)*
Shake a Crooked Town (1960)*
Backfire (1961)
The Name of the Game is Death (1962)
[pub in UK as Operation Overkill, 1973]**
Strongarm (1963)
Never Live Twice (1964)
Death Deep Down (1965)
Four for the Money (1966)
The Vengeance Man (1966)
The Raven is a Blood Red Bird [w/William Odell] (1967)
Route of the Red Gold (1967)
One Endless Hour (1969)
[pub in UK as Operation Endless Hour, 1975]**
Operation Fireball (1969)**
Flashpoint (1970) [pub in UK as Operation Flashpoint, 1972]**
Operation Breakthrough (1971)**
Operation Drumfire (1972)**
Operation Checkmate (1972)**
Operation Stranglehold (1973)**
Operation Whiplash (1973)**
Operation Hammerlock (1974)**
Operation Deathmaker (1975)**
Operation Counterpunch (1976)**

*Johnny Killain series
** Earl Drake series

As by Gar Wilson
Guerilla Games (1982)

www.ingramcontent.com/pod-product-compliance
Lightning Source LLC
Chambersburg PA
CBHW010642100726
47900CB00011B/2941